NOTHING HIDDEN EVER STAYS

HR MASON

NOTHING HIDDEN EVER STAYS

HR MASON

TANGLED TREE
PUBLISHING

For information, contact the publisher, Tangled Tree Publishing.

WWW.TANGLEDTREEPUBLISHING.COM

EDITING: HOT TREE EDITING
DESIGNER: BOOKSMITH DESIGN
FORMATTER RMGRAPHX
E-BOOK ISBN: 9781925853636
PAPERBACK ISBN: 978-1-925853-64-3

DEDICATION

This book is dedicated to my family and friends for always believing in me.

ROSS FAMILY TREE

Cullen Ross (1760-1818) married Ione Fairbairn (1778-1818)
Their children: Marshall and Eleanor

Eleanor Ross (1794-1818)

Marshall Ross (1793-1825) married Marie Stockton (1797-1822)
Their child: Byron

Byron Ross (1821-1861) married Emilia Duncan (1823-1841)
Their child: George

George Ross (1839-1866) married Anne Ashbridge (1845-1866)
Their child: Peter

Peter Ross (1865-1920) married Catherine Sykes (1877-1897)
Their child: Clarence

Clarence Ross (1895-1932) married Elsie Willard (1900-1920)
Their child: James

James Ross (1916-1960) married Annabelle Fraser (1918-1940)
Their child: Stuart

Stuart Ross (1939-1998) married Elizabeth Waterford (1950-2018)
Their child: Anna

Anna Ross (1977-1997) and unknown father
Their child: Aubrey

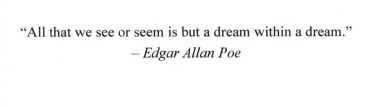

"All that we see or seem is but a dream within a dream."
– *Edgar Allan Poe*

CHAPTER ONE

Seattle, Washington
2019

Aubrey Ross had always suspected she might be a little
unhinged. Not enough to be locked up in the psychiatric
ward, but just enough to understand she was different.
She often felt her grip on reality slipping, ever so slightly,
dangling by a thread, balancing on her fingertips. If she
held on tightly, everything would be just fine. Her façade of
normalcy could continue.

But if she managed to slip, even a little, she would lose
her hold on the present, sliding into the dark, muddled abyss
of her past. She couldn't allow that to happen. The past
was not where she wanted to spend even a second of her
time. Nothing good could come from looking back. And yet
sometimes she did.

When she left work at the diner that evening, Aubrey
wondered if it was her overactive imagination telling her

she was being followed, or if she really was. Sometimes it was hard for her to distinguish between fantasy and reality.

A man dressed in a black trench coat and bowler hat stepped from the shadows behind her and brandished an envelope with her name written in bold black letters. Aubrey gasped, even though she'd known ahead of time that something strange was about to happen. She always knew. Her premonitions were as much a part of her as her sapphire eyes.

"Are you Ms. Aubrey Ross?" The man raised one bushy eyebrow in question.

"Who wants to know?"

She pulled her raincoat around her thin frame and tried to appear larger than she was in case the man intended to harm her.

"I'm Mr. Wilson Wayfair. I've come on behalf of your grandmother," he answered with a tip of his hat.

"You have the wrong Aubrey Ross. I don't have a grandmother. I don't have any family at all," Aubrey replied.

"Oh, but you're wrong. And I've been looking for you for quite some time, Ms. Ross." She glanced at the man, taking stock of his demeanor. He was a peculiar fellow who seemed better suited for a Sherlock Holmes novel than for the streets of Seattle. Between his outdated attire and his handlebar mustache, the man was a walking anachronism. She nearly expected to see him light up a pipe and pull out a magnifying glass for effect.

"You've been looking for me?" she asked.

"I have."

"And why have you been looking for me?" Aubrey was certain the man was lying. She'd been alone her entire life. No one was looking for her. No one ever had been.

"I've been searching for you for a while. You've been a tricky little thing to track down," he chuckled.

"I told you before, you have the wrong girl."

Aubrey nodded curtly and started to walk away. Mr. Wayfair gently placed one hand on her arm to stop her.

"I am very certain you're not the wrong girl. Will you please allow me to explain?"

Something about the way he asked, kindly and respectfully, caused her to stop. In her twenty-five years of life, she'd very rarely been spoken to in such a manner. Not one of her countless foster parents had spoken that way. Her social workers had always been too busy to be anything but abrupt. She'd certainly never experienced any kindness or respect from the employers in any of the run-down diners where she'd worked. It was the man's demeanor that finally convinced her to listen.

"Go ahead," she relented.

"Your grandmother, Elizabeth Ross, passed away six months ago. Her attorney, Andrew Lemon, and I have been trying to find you. Basically we've searched for you ever since your mother—"

"My mother? What do you know about my mother?" Aubrey didn't even try to conceal the anger in her voice.

"I know your mother ran away. I know she was only seventeen when you were born, and she was unable to properly care for you. I know your grandmother wanted you found, and we've done our best to do so," Mr. Wayfair answered gently.

"Did you know my mother abandoned me at a hospital? Did you know she didn't even care enough to keep me? Did you know she left me there at only three years old, with nothing more than a shabby old blanket? Because of her, I became a ward of the state." Aubrey's voice shook as she lashed out at the stranger standing before her.

"I don't pretend to know all the details, but I can imagine your life has been difficult," Mr. Wayfair replied.

"You can't imagine the half of it," she bit back bitterly.

"No, I suppose I can't. I'm unable to comprehend what you might have been through. And I'm sorry for that. But I have some news that might interest you."

"What news?"

In spite of the fact that the mention of her mother brought up memories she'd just as soon forget, she had to admit she was curious. Aubrey was shocked to realize she wanted the man to continue his tale.

"As I said, your grandmother passed away six months ago. With your mother also being deceased, you are the last living member of the Ross family."

Aubrey's eyes widened. "My mother is dead?"

"Yes. I assumed someone would have told you."

"They didn't. Are you sure?" Aubrey had always wondered the fate of the woman who had so easily abandoned her. Sometimes she imagined her mother had gone on to lead a wonderful life filled with other children that she'd wanted. She never imagined for one second that the woman who had given her life was dead.

"Anna Ross died in 1997," Mr. Wayfair explained.

"My mother's name was Anna?"

"Yes, it was."

Aubrey swallowed hard as she digested the information. Knowing her mother's name somehow made everything feel different. It made her real. Up until that moment, she could pretend the woman was fictional, but hearing her name jarred Aubrey to her very core. Her mother had been a living, breathing human, and her name was Anna.

"I don't understand. If she died in 1997, I would have been three. That's how old I was when she left me at the hospital."

"It would seem so."

"How did my mother die?"

Aubrey had so many questions, having lived with unanswered ones her entire life. Mr. Wayfair seemed to have snippets of information regarding her mother, and as much as she wanted to bury the past, she also needed to know.

"Anna Ross was found in a hotel room in Denver in 1997. I'm sorry to be the one to tell you this, Ms. Ross, but your mother hanged herself," he replied quietly as he wiped a stray tear from his eye.

Aubrey gasped. "She killed herself?"

"Yes. She was always a tortured soul."

"What do you mean, she was tortured?"

The idea Mr. Wayfair presented resonated deep within her soul. In the darkest, most hidden recesses of her heart, it was the way Aubrey had always viewed herself. Tortured.

"I knew your mother her entire life, and she was always quite unhappy."

"How so?"

"The only time I remember seeing Anna smile was the last day I saw her, the day she left home. She said, 'Mr. Wayfair, I'm getting out of here. Aubrey and I are leaving this place, and we're never coming back. I don't know if I can save myself, but I have to at least try to save her.' I'll never forget the smile on her beautiful face as she said goodbye."

Aubrey noticed Mr. Wayfair's eyes brimming with unshed tears, and she marveled at the fact that she was standing face-to-face with a person who had known her mother, the woman who had been an enigma, a figment of her imagination. Aubrey often wondered if she'd even been real. But the man in front of her claimed to have known her.

"You said my mother left her home? Where was she from?" Aubrey felt the sudden need to absorb all the man's knowledge about Anna Ross.

"Well, that's why I'm here. This is for you." Mr. Wayfair placed the envelope into her hands.

"What is it?" Aubrey's fingertips caressed the embossed letters that spelled out her name.

"Your inheritance. It's a house in Rossdale, Ohio. The town was named after your ancestors, by the way."

"That's a lot to take in, considering I grew up believing I had no family," she answered, her voice dripping with sarcasm.

"Everything is yours. Inside that envelope is the paperwork you'll need to claim Desolate Ridge, your ancestral estate. You own it. All of it."

"Desolate Ridge? What kind of name is that?" Aubrey smirked.

"I think you'll find the name to be quite fitting," Mr. Wayfair replied under his breath.

Aubrey fidgeted with the envelope, mildly curious but mostly suspicious. Mr. Wayfair expected her to just believe he was telling her the truth? Time and circumstances had taught Aubrey that if something seemed too good to be true, it probably was.

"I'm sorry, sir, but I'm not really interested in a house in Ohio. What would I want with it? I've never even been out of the state of Washington." Aubrey tossed her chestnut curls, her perfect, beautiful face remaining impassive.

"But it's yours. A member of the Ross family has lived in that house since 1819."

The look in the man's eyes was a mixture of hope and desperation. It was almost as if his very existence depended on Aubrey's acceptance of his offering. She had no idea why it meant so much to him, but it didn't matter to her in the slightest.

Aubrey Ross worked a dead-end job, barely scraping by from paycheck to paycheck. That was the way her life had always been, and she had no hope of her situation improving anytime soon. If Mr. Wayfair was counting on her to be financially responsible for anything, he was going to be sorely disappointed.

"Look, I'm sorry you've come all of this way for nothing, but I'm really not interested."

"But, Ms. Ross—"

"I appreciate the information about my mother. It fills in a couple of blanks for me, and I suppose if what you say is true, there might have been a time when she cared for me, even a little. That's something I never had before," Aubrey began.

"Oh, my dear, your mother loved you more than life itself."

"What?" Aubrey's heart beat faster as she contemplated the man's words. She had constructed an image of the woman who had abandoned her, and it didn't include love. Confusion warred inside her heart. She wanted nothing more than for the painful conversation to end.

"Anna might have been young, but you were her entire world. You gave her hope. You gave her the courage to leave her miserable situation. She did for you what she couldn't do for herself."

Aubrey had the distinct feeling Mr. Wayfair knew far more than he was saying, but she was so overwhelmed by the strange turn of events that she didn't ask him to elaborate. Her brain was trying to process everything she'd learned, and she couldn't do it with a teary-eyed old man staring at her.

"I'm sorry, Mr. Wayfair, but I have to be going."

Aubrey turned on her heel and strode away from the man before he could say anything else about her mother or her apparent inheritance. Her life was a train wreck. It always had been. The last thing she needed was the responsibility of a house in Ohio.

CHAPTER TWO

Rossdale, Ohio
1819

"*This is the last time, Henry. It has to be. If someone were to catch us....*" *Marie Stockton turned away, trying to halt the tears before they fell.*

"*No one will see us. The woods are thick, and I wasn't followed,*" *Henry Metzger replied quickly, trying to convince Marie their whereabouts were unknown.*

Henry pulled Marie close in an effort to comfort her. There was little else he could do. Even though propriety forbade such a blatant show of affection, he didn't care. If he could shield her from the pain, he would. Henry would take Marie's sadness and absorb it into himself. He would do anything to see her smile again.

He remembered the first time he'd met her. She had been so lovely and full of life. Marie's laughter danced across the street to where Henry was standing, grabbing his heart and not letting go. One look at her and Henry had never been the same. He'd had a million dreams of their life together. But it wasn't to be. It couldn't be. Marie's parents had seen to that.

"When is the wedding?" Henry's voice cracked on the last word. He couldn't imagine the woman he loved marrying someone else, let alone that beast Marshall Ross.

"In two months. Marshall says we will be married once the house is built," Marie answered sadly.

"That house is a monstrosity."

"I know it is," Marie whispered.

Henry gritted his teeth. He should have been proud of Desolate Ridge, as the house had been named. After all, he was the foreman of the building crew. The house would be brought into existence because of him. Every brick that made up the home would bear his fingerprint. Each nail would be hammered into the foundation under his watchful eye.

It was to be the grandest, most beautiful house in the entire state. But the thought of Marie living there with Marshall Ross was enough to turn his stomach. He couldn't bear it. He had to do something.

The wind rustled the leaves on the trees, moaning and wailing loudly, like a newborn baby. Henry pulled his wool tailcoat a bit closer to his body.

Marie shivered. Her walking dress and pelisse offered much-needed warmth, but the chill originated from deep within, and no amount of velvet could chase it away. She'd felt cold and dead inside ever since the day her parents told her the news that would forever change the trajectory of her life.

Perhaps she should have been honored to be the chosen bride of Marshall Ross, the wealthiest man in Ohio. A lot of girls in her position would have been pleased. The Stockton family wasn't affluent, so the prospect of a man of Marshall's standing taking an interest in Marie should have been flattering.

She knew Marshall's interest had nothing to do with her character or virtue and everything to do with her beauty. He believed he should have the loveliest woman in town, and that was Marie. Marshall said her chestnut curls and sapphire eyes had captivated him with only a glance. He'd known in an instant that she belonged to him.

For the first time in her life, Marie cursed her face, wishing she'd been born with an unremarkable countenance. Her loveliness had betrayed her, her beauty sentencing her to a life she'd never wanted.

Her parents had been celebrating for weeks, oblivious to the fact that their daughter grew more despondent by the day. They could see nothing beyond Marshall's wealth, but Marie saw other things, darker things, and the thought of marrying him consumed her thoughts by day and haunted her dreams by night.

She couldn't quite put her finger on it, but something about Marshall terrified her. Maybe it was the fact that his smile never reached his eyes, or that his laughter rang hollow. There appeared to be no emotion in the man whatsoever. His heart seemed a cold, vacant place.

When Marie looked at him, she saw nothing but a deep, dark void. His hands were as cold as ice when he helped her in and out of his carriage, and his touch made her blood run cold. Marie believed he didn't love her so much as he desired to possess and control her. Marshall Ross was a man of secrets, and she was afraid of what she would find once they were unlocked.

There was also the strange disappearance of Marshall's sister, Eleanor. It had happened last spring, right before work began on Desolate Ridge. Eleanor had gone to church one Sunday. She'd walked home alone after services, and she'd never been seen again. It seemed the young woman had simply vanished.

There was talk that Eleanor left Rossdale, the town named after her own family, because she was angry about the house Marshall wanted to build. There were no facts to back up the rumors, only supposition, yet the whispers lingered, hanging in the air like a puff of smoke from her father's pipe.

The idea of Eleanor leaving town was plausible. Considering her wealth, the young woman had the means to go wherever she wished. Mr. and Mrs. Ross had left their children a vast inheritance upon their untimely deaths the previous year. Rumor had it that Marshall and Eleanor were bequeathed millions, and their parents' will stipulated it should be split evenly between the children.

The Ross fortune was larger than anyone in town could fathom. The family's power was even greater, controlling every aspect of Rossdale.

Marie glanced at Henry and thought about how different he was in comparison to her betrothed. She had loved him for years, and they had always intended to marry. Henry was warmth, compassion, comfort, and hope; he was all of the things Marshall Ross was not.

Marie's heart ached to be with Henry, but she had no choice in the matter. Her parents had decided her fate, and they would not entertain any other ideas. Marie's opinion on her future counted for nothing.

"What if we ran away together, Marie?" Henry's deep voice cut into the silence of the woods.

"Ran away?"

"We could leave right now and never come back."

The idea of eloping had been circulating in his mind for weeks, and although he knew it was dangerous, he had no choice but to offer. He wouldn't be able to live with himself if he didn't at least try to change her mind.

"Henry, we can't."

"Yes we can."

"There is nowhere we could go that Marshall wouldn't find us. He is powerful and determined. I will not risk his wrath on you. I love you far too much to put you in jeopardy."

The tears Marie had been trying so desperately to hold back finally broke free and coursed down her face, flowing like the Walhonding River. It was no use. Marshall Ross had made up his mind. He wanted her, and no one could prevent it. No amount of love for Henry could change it, and she would not endanger him to save herself.

"But I love you, Marie. And I fear for you. Something is

not right about that man, or his mansion."

"I know. Every time I see the house, I feel as if someone's hands are on my throat, squeezing, tightening, and stealing my breath."

"What?" Henry's voice registered shock upon hearing Marie's words. He stepped closer to her, tenderly placing his hand on her arm.

"I can't explain it, but it's like Desolate Ridge is alive. And it's warning me." Marie shook her head and forced a small laugh. "It sounds ridiculous when I speak the words out loud."

"I agree. There is something wrong with the house. Every week there is a new accident or strange occurrence at the building site."

"What are you talking about, Henry?"

"The crew tells me about tools disappearing, odd whispers, unexplained voices, and visions of things that aren't there. Marie, I think the house is cursed."

Marie shook her head. "Enough. No more. We mustn't talk of such things."

"Not even if they're true?"

"I need to go now, Henry. This is the last time I will meet you, so please don't ask me again."

"But, Marie—"

"I cannot put myself through the agony any longer. I must accept my fate. I will marry Marshall Ross."

Marie wiped her eyes with the handkerchief Henry offered. She started to give it back to him, then stuffed it into her reticule instead. She would keep it as a memento of what her life might have been. She would need her memories of Henry to make it through the dark days ahead.

"I fear for you, Marie," Henry repeated.

"I fear for myself, and my future children. I worry I won't be able to stop what is coming, and if I can't, the darkness will consume us all. The terror is so strong that some days I feel it strangling me. I pray my trepidation is unfounded."

Before Henry could argue, Marie leaned forward, kissed him softly on the lips, gathered her dress and pelisse into her hands, and dashed through the woods toward home.

CHAPTER THREE

Seattle, Washington
2019

Aubrey wiped down the Formica table where her last customers of the day had just finished eating greasy chicken. She'd worked at the hole-in-the-wall diner for the past year, and she still could not believe people spent their hard-earned paychecks eating the food prepared in that kitchen. She'd never had so much as a salad from the place, always packing and bringing her own lunch from home for her shifts.

She walked to the back room and removed the blue apron from her waist, hanging it on her hook before grabbing her coat and purse and making a quick beeline for the door. She didn't say goodbye to any of her coworkers, and they didn't even bother looking up as she left. It didn't matter; she was there to collect a paycheck, not to make friends.

It wasn't as if Aubrey set out to be rude. Connecting with people didn't come easily to a woman like her. As a ward of the state for most of her life, Aubrey learned early on that opening herself up to others only led to pain and disappointment. She'd been through more foster homes than she could even count, each one worse than the last. Life had taught her to be tough, and she'd figured out the only person she could depend on was herself.

She had no family, not a single friend, and barely any acquaintances. She didn't want them. She was polite and efficient at her job, but aside from that, she made no effort to let anyone behind her wall. She was alone, and she preferred it that way.

Aubrey had been with only two men in her life, and both had crashed and burned, ending in disaster. She wasn't one to point fingers; she knew the fault had been hers, and she placed the blame entirely at her own feet. She was closed off, safely defended behind a barricade of her own construction. If a person attempted to get too close, she shut them down. Aubrey believed it was always best to end things first, because eventually everyone left. It hurt less if you were the one who did the leaving.

In typical Seattle fashion, it was raining. It wasn't a downpour but was just enough of a mist to dampen her cheeks and cause her unruly curls to frizz. Aubrey pulled the hood of her raincoat over her head and walked briskly toward her apartment. She lived just two blocks from work, which was convenient. It was one of the only perks she could find in either her shabby apartment or her dead-end job.

"Excuse me, Ms. Ross. Can I please speak with you?"

She immediately recognized the voice behind her to be that of Mr. Wilson Wayfair. Aubrey stopped abruptly and turned to face the man.

"You just don't give up, do you? I figured you'd be on a plane on your way back to Ohio by now," she said with a shake of her head.

"I can't leave until I convince you to go to Rossdale."

There was a sense of determination in his voice that hadn't been there the day before.

"But I already told you I'm not interested. Why won't you just leave me alone?"

"I can't. The house is yours," he insisted.

Water droplets beaded on the brim of his bowler hat. Aubrey watched as the rain collected at the edge, preparing to drip onto the lapel of his trench coat.

"Mr. Wayfair, in case you haven't noticed, I live in Washington," she stated with a sigh.

"You could just as easily live in Ohio. In the house that belongs to you. You have nothing to hold you here," he replied.

"How do you know what I have?" Aubrey thought Mr. Wayfair was an awfully presumptuous man to assume she could just pack up her life at a moment's notice.

"I've done my homework. I told you I've searched for you for a very long time, and now that I've found you, I'm not giving up until you go to Ohio and claim what is rightfully yours."

He set his jaw. It was easy to see the strange man could be very stubborn when the mood struck.

"What's in it for you? Why do you care so much about my inheritance?"

He paused, his face progressing through a myriad of emotions until finally landing somewhere between melancholy and wistfulness.

"It's my job to care. I've worked for the Ross family for many years. I wish to see Desolate Ridge in the hands of its rightful owner. I wish for things to finally be made right."

Aubrey knew there was more to his story, but she didn't push him. She had the feeling he would eventually share the real reason behind his mission to see her claim her birthright, so she waited silently until he continued.

"You see, Ms. Ross, I felt a sort of grandfatherly attachment to your mother. I never had children of my own, and I always had a soft spot for Anna. I didn't do enough for her... didn't help her when she needed it most. I'd hoped she would find happiness somehow, but she couldn't escape the monsters inside herself. If I can help you, it will almost be as if I've helped Anna," he said with a shrug.

"Well, Mr. Wayfair, that's a nice sentiment, but even if I wanted to go, I don't have the money to fly to Ohio," Aubrey replied matter-of-factly.

"Oh, money isn't a concern that you need to have." Mr. Wayfair chuckled as if he were privy to some humorous joke Aubrey knew nothing about.

"I assure you money is a concern I've always had, seeing as I don't have any."

Aubrey crossed her arms and narrowed her eyes at the man. He must not know as much about her as he claimed.

If he did, he'd know she was basically penniless.

"Ms. Ross, as I've said, money isn't a concern. You may not have had it before, but it won't ever be a problem for you again."

"I don't believe you," she countered.

"Perhaps this will convince you. It has been worn by the mistress of Desolate Ridge for generations. Marshall Ross, the man who built the house, gave it to his wife, Marie, on their wedding day. It has been passed down to every Ross woman ever since."

Mr. Wayfair reached into his pocket and presented Aubrey with the largest sapphire ring she'd ever seen. It was clearly an antique, and the blue stone was the exact color of her eyes. Her hand trembled as she opened her palm and Mr. Wayfair plunked the piece of jewelry into it. Mesmerized, she slid the ring onto her finger. It fit perfectly, almost as if it were custom-made for her.

It stopped raining, so Aubrey removed her hood and shook out her hair. She nibbled nervously on the skin around her fingernails, which was a nasty habit she'd developed as a young girl and had never outgrown. She shivered as she felt the brush of a fingertip on her cheek and the sound of a woman crying.

Aubrey whipped her head around, certain someone was standing behind her. When she turned, she saw no one but Mr. Wayfair, who appeared unruffled by the sound. He clearly hadn't heard the woman crying, or felt the brush of someone's fingertip.

Goose bumps erupted on her arms, and the hairs on

the back of her neck prickled. Her eye twitched, and she shivered. It wasn't particularly cold outside, but Aubrey was chilled to the bone.

Experiencing a physical reaction due to an unexplained feeling or occurrence was a phenomenon she'd lived with her entire life. Aubrey couldn't explain it, but she had felt *something*. Oblivious, Mr. Wayfair reached into the inside pocket of his trench coat and pulled out another envelope, this one much thicker than the one he'd given her the previous night. When he placed it into her hands, it was heavy.

"What's this?" she asked.

"I told you I've done my homework. I knew you wouldn't have the means to travel, Ms. Ross, so I came prepared."

"Prepared? What do you mean?"

"I withdrew a small amount of cash from your family's account before I left Ohio. It should be more than enough to cover your travel expenses," he clarified.

Aubrey slowly opened the envelope and looked inside. There were several stacks of cash, bundled into little piles. She flipped through them, noticing each stack was made up of hundred-dollar bills. She gasped and searched Mr. Wayfair's face for an explanation. She'd never seen that much money in her life.

"How much is in there?"

"I only brought ten thousand with me. I figured that would be enough to cover whatever you might need until you arrive in Ohio." He answered nonchalantly, as if he'd handed her a twenty-dollar bill.

"You're telling me there's ten thousand dollars in this envelope?" Aubrey knew her eyes were probably the size of dinner plates, but she couldn't help it.

"Ms. Ross, I don't think you fully understand what I'm trying to explain. You are the sole owner of Desolate Ridge and the beneficiary of the entire Ross family fortune. The money you're holding right now is a mere drop in the bucket. You are a very, very rich woman." He smiled.

Aubrey felt faint. Surely there must have been some mistake. She had lived her entire life below the poverty line, and this strange-looking man was telling her she was rich? Something didn't add up. There had to be a catch, some sort of caveat Mr. Wayfair wasn't disclosing.

"I'm sure this is surprising news, but you'll find it is all true. The Ross family fortune is vast, and it's all yours. The house, the stocks, the jewelry, the cars, all of the bank accounts—everything. All you have to do is go to Ohio and claim it," he encouraged.

"What if I don't want the house?"

"What are you talking about? Why wouldn't you want the house?"

"If it's mine, I can just sell it, right?"

Aubrey had no desire to live in Ohio, but if what Mr. Wayfair said was true, she could sell the house and keep the money. No matter how she looked at the situation, it was worth a trip to the middle of nowhere.

"Ms. Ross, as I've told you, Desolate Ridge has been in your family since 1819. I promise that once you're there, you'll never leave."

CHAPTER FOUR

Desolate Ridge
Rossdale, Ohio
1822

Marie held her son tightly to her chest as she rocked back and forth and hummed quietly. The baby was finally quiet, although the respite wouldn't last long. She breathed a sigh of relief. It seemed nothing she tried would soothe her boy. He'd been crying for months, and Marie was exhausted.

To say Byron Ross was a fussy baby would have been an extreme understatement. Both Marie and the baby nurse tried everything to calm him but to no avail. The doctor assured the frazzled mother there was nothing wrong with her child, but Marie knew better. Her baby was unhappy and discontented, and he refused to be pacified. Something wasn't right.

Her husband, Marshall, told her to stop coddling him. He demanded she give their son to the nurse and forget about him, saying she had more important matters with which to concern herself. The mistress of Desolate Ridge was supposed to be beautiful and regal, not exhausted and depressed. He told her if she were a better mother, and a better wife, none of it would have happened. But she didn't care about any of that. All she wanted was for the baby to stop crying.

Marshall warned Marie that his patience was wearing thin. He told her if she didn't take care of the situation, he would do so himself. She believed her husband, which was why she rarely slept. His threats and the insanity she saw so clearly behind his eyes were the very reasons she feared for her life. Marshall told Marie on their wedding day that he didn't intend to share her with anyone, not even their children.

Marie's role was to bear the offspring who would carry on the Ross name. It wasn't her job to worry about mundane details like raising them. Her only task was to be an ornamental fixture. He'd married her because she was beautiful, not because she was maternal. He'd hired the nurse to care for their son, and he made sure his wife understood her loyalty was only to him. She was his property, his to do with as he pleased.

Marie had tried to be a good wife. She'd tried to do what her husband demanded. She'd had every intention of handing the child over to the nurse once he was born. But the moment Marie held her son in her arms, she'd been unable to give him up. She wanted nothing more than to love and protect him.

So she'd defied Marshall every single day for the past four months of Byron's life. She rocked her son, she sang to him, she rarely left his side, and she begged him to stop crying. She did all she could to calm him, but nothing worked.

It was almost as if the infant were tortured by some inner turmoil. In the moments when desperation and exhaustion took over, Marie wondered if her son had inherited the madness of his father. God help them all if he had. Marshall's insanity grew like the winding ivy that crept up the side of Desolate Ridge, choking out everything in its path. There was a monster lurking just below the surface of her husband, a savage beast disguised as a handsome, distinguished gentleman.

In the darkest, most secret places of her heart, Marie feared her husband's affliction may have been passed on to their son.

On one occasion, shortly after the wedding, Marie had dared to question Marshall on a seemingly trivial matter. Without warning, he flew into a rage, throwing his crystal scotch tumbler across the room and shattering it into a million pieces. He'd grabbed her wrist, dragged her up the winding staircase to the attic, flung her onto the floor, and locked her inside. Marie was stunned, but it all happened so quickly she'd barely had time to react.

Marshall imprisoned her in the attic for a week. He only released her when she grew ill, and upon an examination by the doctor, discovered she was with child. Producing heirs was Marshall's highest goal, so he'd allowed Marie to return to her room in order to ensure the safety of the child.

Marie had suspected Marshall was unkind before they

were married, but it went much deeper than that. He wasn't only unkind; he was evil. She locked her door tightly on the nights when she dared to sleep. Most nights she sat with Byron in the attic, alert yet exhausted, wary and waiting.

She didn't know exactly what she was waiting for, but she knew it was coming. She knew it as sure as she knew her own name. Marie thought of Henry Metzger, dear, sweet Henry, who would have loved and cherished her and their children. How different her life might have been!

Marie kissed the top of her son's downy head and whispered that she loved him. She dreamed of running away, but there was nowhere they could go that Marshall wouldn't find them. She stroked her baby's back and the glint of the moonlight streaming in through the window reflected off the large sapphire wedding ring that had been placed on her finger. That ring had sealed her fate.

Marie Ross knew the darkness was coming for her, and there was no way she could stop it, no place she could go to escape. Her only comfort was in knowing Marshall wanted heirs, so Byron would be safe. She, however, was dispensable. There was no hope for her.

Marie could feel the shadows closing in, creeping slowly day by day. They wrapped their spindly fingers around her neck, squeezing tightly like a vise. She knew she could struggle, but she would not prevail. Marie understood that one day there would be no breath left.

CHAPTER FIVE

Aubrey adjusted her weary body in the airplane seat. She'd never flown before because she couldn't afford it. The irony wasn't lost on her that her inaugural flight happened to be in the first-class cabin of the plane. Mr. Wayfair had purchased her ticket and provided directions on what to do once she landed in Ohio. A driver would meet her at the airport and escort her to Desolate Ridge. Mr. Wayfair had tipped his hat and waved goodbye to Aubrey at the gate. She'd assumed he would fly back to Rossdale with her, but apparently he had other work to attend to.

It was hard to believe only two days had passed since she'd heard the news that would forever change her life. She was no longer Aubrey Ross, orphaned, abandoned, penny-pinching waitress. She was Aubrey Ross, multibillionaire and mistress of Desolate Ridge. It was a lot to wrap her head around, but once the shock wore off, she'd enjoyed quitting her job and turning in the key to her dumpy apartment.

Aubrey didn't know what awaited her in Ohio. All she

knew was it had to be better than what she'd left behind in Seattle. Besides, she didn't intend to stay. She would make a plan to prepare the house to be sold, and she would decide where to go after that. If she were truly as wealthy as Mr. Wayfair said, she could go anywhere in the world.

She grabbed her purse and rifled through its contents, resting her fingertips on the object of her search. Before she'd boarded the plane, Mr. Wayfair handed her yet another envelope and asked her to open it once she was in the air. Aubrey was curious, but she'd lived her entire life not knowing her family's secrets, so she'd agreed not to look at it right away.

The pilot announced the aircraft had reached its cruising altitude, so she decided it was an acceptable time to discover the envelope's contents. She slid open the seal, reached inside, and pulled out a letter. As soon as her fingertips touched the paper, she felt a current course through her, like a zap of electricity. She jumped, dropped the letter in her lap, and glanced around to see if anyone else had experienced the jolt. No one seemed disturbed but Aubrey.

She grabbed the paper once again, overcome with curiosity, turning it around in her hands. It was worn and crumpled, and the handwriting was sloppy. There was a red sticky note attached that read

This note was found in your mother's room when they recovered her body. I hesitated to show it to you, but I thought it was best for you to know.

The note was signed by Mr. Wayfair.

Aubrey removed the letter and began to read the crooked,

slanted writing.

I believed I could save her. I thought if I left that madhouse, there would be some hope for my daughter. I wanted so badly to give Aubrey the life she deserved. Once again I've failed. It seems like that's all I know how to do. I'm not fit to be anyone's mother. She's better off without me. If she's raised by others, maybe the curse that follows our horrible family will finally be broken. I wish I had been stronger.

— Anna Ross

Aubrey reread the letter three more times. She didn't realize she was crying until a large teardrop splashed onto the paper, causing the ink to run. She couldn't remember the last time she'd cried. It was uncomfortable and strange, and she tried to shut it down, but she couldn't. Instead, she closed her eyes and allowed Anna's final words to sink in. She felt them chipping away, just a little, permeating the hard outer shell she'd grown for self-preservation.

She'd spent her life trying not to feel anything. Emotions were nothing but barriers to survival. She'd made it through the foster care system by being numb, had mastered the skill. Yet there she was, weeping over a letter written by the woman who had abandoned her. She was crying over desperate words written by Anna Ross before she'd hanged herself.

Aubrey had concocted an image of her mother as a terrible girl who had been too selfish for motherhood, imagining her to be a junkie or a drunk. She'd pictured her leaving her child at the hospital without a moment's hesitation. She had lived with the idea of this imaginary mother, who grew more despicable as the years passed. Never for a second had Aubrey considered that the woman who abandoned her might be anything but reprehensible.

As she read the letter and considered the words, a tiny sliver of something she didn't understand crept inside. It wasn't love; Aubrey didn't believe herself to be capable of that emotion. She could never love her mother, but maybe she could understand what Anna might have been feeling. Maybe she could believe that Anna was trying to do the right thing. Maybe she could sympathize with a girl who was damaged and tormented, just as she was.

Maybe....

Aubrey wiped her face and gently folded the letter, returning it to the envelope in her purse. She didn't know why Mr. Wayfair had decided to share it with her, but she was glad he did. It couldn't heal the hurt, not even close, but somehow it helped.

If nothing else, her curiosity was piqued. She wanted to know more about her mother, the Ross family, Desolate Ridge, and the supposed curse. Perhaps whetting her appetite had been the strange man's plan all along.

Aubrey closed her eyes and rested her head on the airplane seat, fidgeting with the large sapphire ring on her hand. When she'd first slipped the ring onto her finger, it fit perfectly. Now it seemed much tighter, almost as if her finger had grown, or the ring had shrunk. She tried to pull it off, but it wouldn't budge. She figured her hands were probably swollen from the change in altitude and left it alone.

Aubrey was tired, and there were several hours remaining on the flight. She didn't know what else to do, so she decided she would sleep. Before long, Aubrey had fallen into a deep slumber. A dream began to spread itself into her subconscious, melting into her mind like snowflakes on warm ground.

The dream began in darkness. She didn't know where she was, but soft moonlight filtered in through the window. Aubrey glanced at her arms. She held a small baby close to her chest as she rocked gently and hummed quietly. The voice was hers, but not quite.

Aubrey knew she wasn't fully herself in the dream, and yet somehow she was. She stroked the baby's back, and the large, sapphire ring glinted in the moon's luminescence. She inhaled the sweet scent of the infant in her arms, and a wave of sadness and desperation cascaded over her like a waterfall. A door creaked open behind her, and footsteps echoed in the quiet room. She gasped, although somehow she'd known he was coming.

The man walked briskly toward her. He pulled the baby from her arms and placed him in the crib across the room. The child wailed, and her heart broke. Deep inside, she knew it was the last time she would hold him. She pleaded with the man, but her words couldn't permeate his insanity.

His face contorted with rage. He leaned in closely, and she smelled the scotch on his breath. His black, soulless eyes were nothing but a void. She began to scream, but the sound was muffled as he wrapped his hands around her neck, squeezing tightly with his fingers.

She couldn't breathe. She'd known the end was coming, and yet she was powerless to stop it. He compressed her neck like a piece of wood in a vise. Her breath grew shallow until it wasn't there at all.

Aubrey awoke, gasping for air like a drowning woman. She breathed in deeply, feeling as if she'd never get enough oxygen. Hands shaking, she touched her neck. Her skin felt warm, almost as if the fiery heat of the man's fingers still lingered.

Her heart pounded wildly. She'd never experienced such a vivid dream. It was ridiculous, but she felt as if the woman was her. She didn't recognize the man, but she knew she would never forget his face.

CHAPTER SIX

Still shaken from the nightmare, Aubrey waited for her luggage at baggage claim. She'd spent the rest of the monotonous flight vacillating between trying to recall every detail of the dream and trying to forget it. The ordeal had been vivid and real, like nothing she'd ever experienced. She was unsure what to make of it, and she hoped it never happened again.

After collecting her bag, she headed toward the terminal and looked around. Mr. Wayfair told her a driver would be there to escort her to Desolate Ridge, but she had no idea how she was supposed to find him. She quickly discovered there was no need to worry when an older man, dressed smartly in a suit, black tie, and driving cap, approached her and reached for her bag.

"How was your flight, Ms. Ross? My name is Carlton, and I'm your driver."

She was a bit taken aback. She had no idea how the stranger knew who she was.

"It was... fine... good, I guess. How do you know who I am?"

"I'd know you anywhere, ma'am. You look just like...."

Carlton's voice trailed off, disappearing into the jumble of sounds in the airport. Aubrey knew he wanted to say more, but something stopped him.

"Who do I look like?" she coaxed, hoping the man would elaborate.

"No one, ma'am. You only have the one bag?"

Carlton avoided her gaze and began walking toward the parking lot. She followed closely behind.

"Yes, sadly, one bag holds all of my worldly possessions," she answered.

"Not anymore, ma'am," he reminded her.

"I suppose you're right."

The pair arrived at a vehicle, a classic Bentley Touring Limousine, and Carlton opened the back door. She'd never seen such a fancy car, and she had to remind herself that it was hers. She wasn't sure what the proper protocol might be, so she hesitated.

Carlton gave her a crooked smile and gestured for her to get into the car. Completely out of her element, Aubrey obeyed. He closed her door, deposited her lone suitcase into the trunk, and slid behind the wheel.

"You should relax, ma'am. It's about an hour and a half to Rossdale. There is a light snack and some drinks in the back, so help yourself. I thought you might be hungry from the flight," Carlton said pleasantly.

"Th-thank you," she stammered.

It didn't take long for Aubrey to discover that Carlton was a man of few words. The pair rode in silence for many miles. Not knowing what to say, and seeing as how she despised small talk, Aubrey relegated herself to staring out the window, watching as the scenery flew by.

She was surprised at the stark difference in the landscape. Seattle was a constant buzz of people, a hubbub of activity, a difficult place to ever be completely alone. Ohio seemed to be its antithesis. Rolling land stretched for miles, wide open, spread out, and lush in its simplicity. Something about the surroundings called out to her, almost as if the countryside were welcoming her home to a place she'd never before been.

They didn't pass through a single metropolis on the entire drive. Farms were scattered here and there across the countryside, and sometimes there were quaint little towns, which were sprinkled with a few homes and small businesses. But that was it. Aubrey wondered about the people who made their lives in such places, far away from the hustle and bustle of a large city. She'd never known anything but urban life, so the small-town experience would be new. Aubrey wondered what awaited her in Rossdale.

As fields of corn and soybeans whirred past the window, her troubled mind returned once again to the nightmare she'd had on the plane. Her hands fluttered to her neck as she recalled the feeling of strangulation. She pictured the face of the man in the dream, and she shivered. She felt the weight of the infant in her arms, the desperation of trying to protect him. She twisted the ring on her finger and tried to forget.

"How much longer, Carlton?"

Aubrey was restless, and she needed to move. She wanted to outrun the vivid images that wouldn't leave her mind.

"We're approaching town now, ma'am," Carlton answered.

"Is there a store?"

"There is a small one, ma'am. Is there something you need? I can get it for you."

"If you'll just drive me there before we go to the house, I would appreciate it. I need to grab a few items."

"I can get whatever you need," he repeated.

"That's quite all right, Carlton. I'm used to doing things for myself," she insisted.

"If you say so, ma'am." He nodded.

Aubrey could tell he wanted to complete the task for her, but the idea of someone serving her was both unfamiliar and uncomfortable. Besides, she didn't actually need anything; she mostly wanted to get out of the car, stretch her legs, and gather her wits.

The town's store seemed like a good place to get a feel for Rossdale. She was curious about the people who lived there, in the town named after her family. She was anxious to check out the locals.

They drove down Main Street, right through the center of town, and folks stopped to stare as the shiny vehicle passed by. Carlton pulled into the parking lot of a small brick building called Lawson's General Store.

Before he could get out of the car, Aubrey opened the back door. She noticed the look of irritation that passed over her driver's face, and she felt a bit guilty for going against protocol, but Carlton would figure out sooner or later that she didn't need anyone to do things for her. She could take care of herself.

"I'll be back in a few minutes," she said quickly as she closed the car door.

Aubrey walked inside the small building, and every head in the place swiveled in her direction. The buzz of chatter she'd heard when she entered was replaced with dead silence. No one smiled, and a woman who was standing nearby gathered her small daughter close to her side, as if Aubrey's presence would somehow endanger her child.

Momentarily taken aback by the strange greeting, she didn't allow the passive expression on her face to waver. Aubrey breathed deeply, held her head high, and ambled down the narrow aisles, pretending not to notice that she was something akin to a circus sideshow. She'd been in many uncomfortable situations in her life, and she'd become an expert at disguising her true feelings.

She grabbed a can of chicken noodle soup, a package of crackers, and a bottle of water before making her way to the cash register; she was hungry, and she didn't know if there would be food at the house. She plunked the items onto the counter, steadily holding the gaze of the young cashier, who tried her best not to look away.

"You're new in town." The cashier, whose name tag said Cammie Lawson, raised her voice to barely above a whisper.

"It would seem so," Aubrey replied.

"What brings you to Rossdale?" The cashier lowered her voice even more, as if their communication should remain a secret.

"Family matters," Aubrey answered curtly.

"Where are you staying?"

Aubrey didn't know if all small-town residents were this invasive, or if it was a phenomenon specific to Rossdale. Either way, she didn't like it.

"I'm staying at Desolate Ridge."

Aubrey purposely answered loud enough for everyone in the store to hear. If they were going to stare, she would give them a good reason.

"Desolate Ridge?"

Cammie's hands trembled as she counted back Aubrey's change.

"Yes, Desolate Ridge. I assume you've heard of it."

"You mean Murder Ridge?"

Aubrey pivoted at the sound of the voice behind her. It came from a tall, angry-looking, acne-faced teenage boy.

"Why did you call it Murder Ridge?"

"There's something wrong with the place. That Ross family is crazy. The house is haunted, you know," he answered.

"Hush, Cooper. Don't scare her," Cammie admonished the boy.

"I don't scare easily," Aubrey insisted, maintaining eye contact with Cooper.

"Well, anyway, I apologize for my brother. He doesn't

know when to stop."

"It's true, Cammie. The house *is* haunted. Everyone knows it. She probably knows it too," Cooper countered.

"Actually, I don't know much about the house at all," Aubrey replied.

"What's your name?" Cooper asked as he chewed his gum faster.

"Aubrey Ross."

She emphasized her surname, knowing it would get a rise out of the onlookers. The sound of her voice zapped the silence of the room, vibrating, touching down like a bolt of lightning from the sky. A woman standing nearby gasped loudly. Aubrey glanced back and forth between Cooper and Cammie. The young man took a step away from her, and his sister's face grew pale.

"Your last name's Ross? Does that mean you're crazy too?" Cooper looked her up and down, shifting nervously from one foot to the other.

Aubrey wasn't sure how to respond, because she honestly didn't have a good answer. Maybe she was crazy. She'd certainly considered the possibility.

"You just ignore him, Ms. Ross. Cooper has a big mouth." The cashier gave Aubrey the smallest hint of a smile. "Here's your bag. Welcome to Rossdale."

CHAPTER SEVEN

"Did you find what you needed, ma'am?" Carlton asked as Aubrey slid into the back seat of the vehicle.

"I did," she answered curtly.

She was still reeling from the incident in Lawson's General Store. She hadn't expected anyone to roll out the red carpet for her when she arrived in Rossdale, but she also hadn't imagined her mere presence would terrify the townspeople. Cooper said Desolate Ridge was haunted. He also said the members of the Ross family were insane. The boy's insinuation of hereditary insanity had really struck a nerve with her.

She'd been called some variety of crazy for most of her life. One of her foster mothers had gone so far as to have Aubrey evaluated by a psychiatrist when she made the mistake of revealing she had premonitions. She often knew something bad was going to happen long before it did. The sixth sense had served her well throughout her difficult life, but others were unsettled by her unexplainable knowledge.

Aubrey had also battled paranoia, depression, and anxiety in some form or other for as long as she could remember. No doctor had ever given her a concrete diagnosis, but Aubrey herself had always known she was different. Was it possible the Ross family genes carried a strand of mental illness?

"Carlton, may I ask you something?"

She didn't know how much the stranger might be willing to share, but she had to start somewhere.

"Go ahead, ma'am," he answered.

"When I was in the store, I mentioned I was headed to Desolate Ridge. The strangest thing happened. A boy called it Murder Ridge, and he said the entire Ross family was crazy. Do you know anything about that?"

She watched Carlton's face closely in the rearview mirror. She'd grown adept at reading other people, and she clearly noticed the look of trepidation that passed over the driver's face. He waited a couple of seconds before answering.

"I wouldn't pay too much attention to the things people say. Folks around here have always been jealous of the Ross family's money. They've made up all sorts of tales. It's just a bunch of wagging tongues."

"So, you're telling me there's no truth in what he said?"

"I think it's best to form your own opinions, ma'am," Carlton replied noncommittally.

Aubrey was irritated. He hadn't answered her questions at all, but if there were secrets afoot at Desolate Ridge, she wouldn't rest until she uncovered them.

She decided to approach the situation from another angle.

"Mr. Wayfair said my grandmother died six months ago. What about my grandfather? I don't even know his name."

"Your grandfather's name was Stuart. He passed away in 1998," Carlton answered.

"That's only a year after my mother killed herself. Did you know him?"

Aubrey needed to piece together the broken shards of her family's history if she had any hope of understanding her place in it.

"Yes, I knew your grandfather. I started driving for him when I was just out of high school," he replied.

"What was he like?"

"Stuart Ross was a force. His word was law, and you didn't want to cross him. I learned early on to keep my head down and do my job."

"How did he die?"

"He died in a long-term psychiatric care facility. He was... volatile, to say the least."

It was painfully obvious that Carlton didn't want to reveal any sensitive information about her family. Aubrey needed answers, though, so she persisted.

"And my grandmother? What was she like? How did she die?"

"Everyone was terrified of your grandmother."

Aubrey's eyes widened. "Why?"

"Elizabeth Ross was a shrewd, domineering woman. A person did not want to anger her. Your grandmother wanted things done a certain way, and you didn't question it."

"How did she die?"

"She died at Desolate Ridge six months ago."

"From what?" Aubrey persisted. It was like pulling teeth to get answers from the driver.

"She had been ill for quite some time. The doctors said she had schizophrenia, but Elizabeth insisted she didn't."

"What made the doctors believe she was schizophrenic?" Aubrey knew there was something else Carlton wasn't saying.

"Your grandmother saw and heard things that weren't really there," Carlton explained.

Aubrey shivered as she digested the news that her grandmother might have had premonitions, just like she did. She ruminated on the fact that her grandfather died in a mental hospital. Every scrap of information she'd gleaned about her family was cryptic and unhappy, prompting even more questions. Her mother had written about trying to outrun a family curse. Aubrey didn't believe in such things, but it did make her wonder.

"There it is, ma'am. That's Desolate Ridge right ahead," Carlton said quietly.

Aubrey glanced out the window as a large creaking wrought iron gate slid open. The car crept up a serpentine road, gravel crunching beneath the tires. Thick trees obscured Aubrey's view of Desolate Ridge, but as they neared the end of the driveway, she saw it.

Silhouetted against the stark gray sky, the house immediately pulled her forward, as if there were a magnetic force field drawing her in. She couldn't have turned back if she wanted to.

The Bentley came to a halt in the circular drive. Aubrey gazed out the car's window, her breath coming in short, rapid bursts. She couldn't move. For a moment, everything stood still, almost as if Aubrey and the house itself had been frozen in time, fossilized inside a chunk of translucent amber.

Desolate Ridge looked more like a fortress than a house. It was a mammoth two-story Federal-style brick mansion, equally imposing and inviting. Her eyes were drawn to the elliptical fanlight and side windows that adorned the large front entrance. The setting sun glinted off the tracery, creating a delicate branching pattern. It was as if a magical spell were being cast by the weblike etchings in the glass.

Nine large Palladian windows adorned the brick façade. At the front of the house was a portico supported by four large columns. Two giant chimneys peeked out of the roof, standing like soldiers at attention, flanked by double garret windows. A pentagonal projection jutted out from the right side of the house, breaking up the dwelling's otherwise perfect symmetry. The side addition of the home also had a porch and several windows.

Emotions Aubrey barely recognized warred inside of her. Longing, fear, desperation, and confusion spun around like a carousel in her brain. The feeling of finally coming home clashed with the clawing need to flee. As Aubrey looked at Desolate Ridge, she fidgeted with the ring, which had once again grown snug on her finger.

As if in a trance, she opened the door of the car and climbed out. She walked slowly across the driveway toward the house. As she approached the front portico, her chest grew tight, gripping, seizing, making her feel as if she couldn't breathe.

Aubrey's icy hands fluttered to her throat, and she recognized the impression of burning fingertips squeezing tightly, exactly as she'd felt in the nightmare. Panic seized her as she struggled to catch her breath. Then, just as quickly as it had come, the sense of suffocation left her, and Aubrey's respiration returned to normal.

She didn't know what was happening. Nothing about the situation made sense.

Aubrey edged closer to the house, and as she did, she glanced up at the garret windows. She blinked twice, certain she was seeing things.

Standing behind the glass of the attic window was a woman in a flowing white gown. Her chestnut hair was the same color as Aubrey's, but it was much longer. It cascaded in waves down her back and spilled like a waterfall over her shoulders.

Aubrey continued to stare, and the woman's sapphire eyes, exactly like her own, bored into her. In the silence of the encroaching darkness, the clear, comprehensible sound of a woman's voice said, "Welcome home."

Spinning around to see who had spoken, Aubrey found there was no one in sight but Carlton, who remained inside the car. When she glanced back toward the attic window, the woman was gone.

CHAPTER EIGHT

Clearly unaware of Aubrey's strange experience, Carlton jumped out of the car, removed the suitcase from the trunk, and walked to the front door of the house. Aubrey tried to regain her composure, but her head was pounding, and she felt faint.

There was no mistaking the fact that Aubrey had clearly heard a voice, and a woman who was her doppelgänger had been standing at the attic window. It must have been real; it was too vivid to have been imagined. Aubrey replayed the scene over again in her mind. There must have been some logical explanation.

Carlton hadn't mentioned whether or not other people lived at Desolate Ridge. Perhaps she wasn't the only one who would be residing in the large house. Maybe the woman also lived there. If so, it would all make perfect sense.

Aubrey followed Carlton through the front door as he flipped on the entry lights. A crystal chandelier illuminated the large central hall. Aubrey gasped at the splendor of the house. There was a large curved spiral staircase winding its way to a second-story landing area. Between the gleaming hardwood floors sprinkled with immense Persian throw rugs and the decorative window caps and rosette moldings throughout the room, Desolate Ridge was the textbook definition of classically refined ornamentation and elegance. The home may have been two centuries old, but its care and upkeep were unrivaled.

"Carlton, does someone else live here? A woman, perhaps?" Aubrey's voice echoed in the vast expanse of the room.

"No, ma'am. It's been empty since your grandmother died."

"Empty?"

"Yes. Mr. and Mrs. Bonaventure and their son, Anson, are the caretakers. They come around every day to work on the grounds and tidy up the house."

"But they're not here now?"

"Right now there's no one here but us," he explained.

Aubrey frowned. "Just us? You're sure?"

"It's just us, ma'am."

"Do you live here?"

"Oh, no, I don't live here. My wife and I live just down the road. But you can call me anytime you need to go somewhere and I'll drive you," he replied.

"Can't I drive myself?"

Aubrey couldn't imagine calling another person whenever she wanted to leave the house. She was fully capable of driving, as long as she had a car and a set of keys.

"Well, you can drive yourself if you'd like, but that's what I'm here for. That's my job. The Ross family members never drive themselves anywhere."

"Well, Carlton, I think you're going to find I'm a bit different from what you're used to."

Carlton seemed bothered by the prospect of her driving. Maybe he was concerned for his job security.

"Is there another car?" she asked. "I don't mind driving myself every now and then."

The driver sighed deeply. Clearly she'd said something wrong.

"Ma'am, there are four cars besides the Bentley in the garage. The keys are hanging in the kitchen. They're all labeled. They all belong to you, so you may do as you wish."

Aubrey had never owned a car. She couldn't afford it. The prospect of owning five of them was unimaginable. The only reason she'd even gotten a driver's license was because she'd lived with a foster mother who taught her to drive when she turned sixteen. She'd wanted Aubrey to drive her own brood of children around, so she'd been happy to have another driver in the house.

"Thank you for the information, Carlton. And don't worry, I will be sure to call you every now and then," she assured him.

"As you wish, ma'am. Is there anything else?"

"Anything else?"

"That you need."

"I don't know. I don't think so."

"Then I'd best be going. My wife will have supper waiting,"

Carlton replied.

"You're leaving? What… I mean, I don't… really know what I'm supposed to do."

Aubrey hadn't thought ahead to what would happen once she arrived. She'd assumed there would be someone there to explain what came next, someone to help her. She was in a strange place, an unfamiliar house, and it was dark outside. She didn't know where to find anything. She didn't know how to get anywhere.

Aubrey had no idea how to be the mistress of an estate. There were rules and customs she couldn't even fathom. There was decorum and etiquette she didn't know, obligations and conventions she didn't understand. She hadn't been raised to take over an empire. She was a foundling; she wasn't groomed for such a role.

"I left Mr. Lemon's card on the kitchen counter," Carlton told her. "That's the door to the right, just down the hall. You should call him soon."

"Why should I call him?"

"He's the Ross family's attorney. He'll be able to better direct you," he deflected.

"What about Mr. Wayfair? When will I see him?"

As anxious as the strange Mr. Wayfair had been for her to claim her inheritance, she'd expected he would remain by her side through everything. He had been annoying, but at that moment she wished he were there.

"Mr. Wayfair is a very busy man. He comes and goes as he pleases. I'm sure he'll be in touch. Call me if you need anything. My number is programmed into the phone in the kitchen. It's labeled as well."

Carlton smiled, tipped his hat, and left.

The thud of the heavy wooden door reverberated in the empty room. Once again, Aubrey was alone, just as she'd always been. She was alone in a mansion that had her name on the deed. She was alone with the ghosts of a past she didn't understand. She was alone with a possible apparition in the attic. She was all alone, while her tenuous grip on reality diminished by the minute.

She listened as the sound of silence settled in all around her. The stillness was deafening. A creaking sound caused the hairs on her arms to stand on end. Her heart raced as the soft fall of footsteps shuffled across the floorboards above. Beads of perspiration pooled on her upper lip.

Aubrey jumped at the loud chiming of the grandfather clock in the hallway. She watched as the large pendulum swung back and forth inside the glass. She told herself her imagination was carrying her away on flights of fancy. She needed to get a grip on reality. She'd imagined the wraith in the window, the voice speaking to her, and the footsteps above. None of it was real.

Glancing at the clock once again, she tried to anchor herself in the present. Time was real; her fabrications were not. Counting each sound of the clock's knell, she realized it was only seven, even though it was already pitch black outside. It seemed much later.

Aubrey's body was weary and her mind was overworked. She didn't know what to do with herself, all alone in the grand house, with nothing but countless hours stretching before her.

She glanced up the large staircase, and shadows danced before her eyes. She thought she saw something move, but she looked away quickly, unable to deal with it. She just needed to take things one step at a time. Aubrey wanted to explore the second floor, but she opted to wait until daylight. Although she hated to admit it, she was spooked.

She wandered down the hall in search of the kitchen, flipping on every light along the way in an effort to chase away the darkness. She saw Mr. Lemon's business card lying on the counter and decided she would call him soon. She didn't have a clue what she was doing, and she was going to need help.

Aubrey had planned on heating up the chicken noodle soup for dinner but suddenly realized she was more tired than hungry. She explored the remaining rooms on the ground floor, discovering each one was more beautiful and grand than the last. She turned on the light in every room as she entered. By the time she ended her tour of the ground floor, the entire lower level of Desolate Ridge was illuminated.

Exhaustion was creeping in like a dense fog, but Aubrey was afraid to go upstairs to find a bedroom. Instead, she wandered back into the parlor. There was a small sofa, and while it didn't appear to be particularly comfortable, it was where she decided she would spend the night.

She curled into a ball, draped the velvet throw blanket over her body, and closed her tired eyes. Before long, she was fast asleep.

She sank quickly into the dream. At first it seemed she was looking at her own reflection in a mirror, but when she peered more closely, she realized it was someone else. The woman was nearly identical to Aubrey in every way, but her clothing and hairstyle were from a different era. She reached out and caressed Aubrey's cheek. A sapphire ring, identical to the one Aubrey wore, glittered in the darkness.

"It all ends with you," the woman whispered as tears coursed down her face.

Aubrey awakened with a start as she heard a loud knock on the front door. She wasn't sure what to do, as she hadn't expected guests. She felt frazzled and disheveled, certainly not up for entertaining.

Jumping to her feet quickly, she smoothed down her wayward curls and opened the front door. Standing before her was a man dressed in a sheriff's uniform.

He was about her age, a head taller, sporting broad shoulders. He had shortly cropped sandy-blond hair, his chiseled jawline covered with scruffy facial hair of the same hue. The man's handsome face created an attractive canvas for his jade-green eyes. His deep voice startled her, and she realized she was staring.

"Is everything all right, ma'am?"

"Everything is fine."

He raised a brow. "You're sure?"

"Of course I'm sure. May I help you with something?"

Aubrey had no idea why the sheriff was there. His presence caught her off guard, but at least he'd interrupted her disturbing dream.

"A neighbor noticed all of the lights were on. I wanted to check things out. No one has lived here for several months."

"I'm... well, I suppose I'm the new owner. My name is Aubrey Ross."

"Well, it's nice to meet you. I'm Hank Metzger, the sheriff of Rossdale."

He gestured to his badge and gave her a lopsided grin. She noticed his teeth were slightly crooked, which suited him. His face would have been far too perfect otherwise.

"Was there something else you needed, Sheriff?"

Aubrey had no idea why, but she felt defensive. She was out of her element, uncomfortable in the strange house, and scared out of her wits to be alone. But she didn't want him to know that. She was no damsel in distress.

"I just wanted to be sure that everything was okay," he replied.

"Everything is just fine."

She didn't return his smile. She took a step away from him and placed her hand on the door, a gesture that it was time for him to go.

"Here's my card. You be sure to call me if you need anything. Being in a strange place can be a bit overwhelming."

Hank handed her a business card and smiled again.

"Thank you. I can take care of myself," she said curtly.

"I have no doubt you can. I'm sure I'll see you around."

He gave her a long, lingering look before smiling again and returning to his patrol car. Aubrey shut the door tightly and locked it. She was about to return to her spot on the couch when a loud crash sounded from the kitchen.

She panicked. Someone was in the house, and she'd just sent the sheriff away.

Aubrey grabbed a heavy ornate candlestick holder from the table beside the front door and crept slowly toward the kitchen. She tiptoed down the hall and poked her head inside the doorway, then raised the candlestick holder above her head and stepped into the room, ready to attack whoever was there.

The sound of a meow took her by surprise. There was a fluffy black cat standing on the countertop, peering over the edge at the bowl that had toppled over the precipice. The animal turned and stared at her, its golden yellow eyes glinting with mischief.

Relief washed over her. She walked slowly toward the feline, hoping not to spook it as she placed her makeshift weapon on the counter. Reaching a tentative hand forward, she gently stroked the animal's inky fur. Rather than running away, the cat plopped down and purred quietly.

"Hello there, where did you come from?"

Her voice sounded inordinately loud in the quiet room. She noticed a name tag attached to the cat's collar.

"Your name is Spectre? Someone clearly had a sense of humor."

The animal appeared to be well cared for and perfectly content in its surroundings. Carlton had mentioned caretakers, so she imagined they were the ones looking after it. She wasn't completely alone in the house after all.

"I know we just met, Spectre, and I'd like to be better company, but I'm tired. We'll chat more tomorrow."

She returned to the sofa, pulled the blanket over her body once again, and drifted off to sleep in the well-lit parlor of Desolate Ridge. It wasn't long before Spectre curled up in a ball beside her.

CHAPTER NINE

It was morning. Thankfully Aubrey had spent the remainder of the night in restful slumber, blissfully uninterrupted by strange dreams of women who looked like her.

She yawned and stretched on the couch. She smiled when she noticed Spectre curled up beside her, quietly watching.

"Good morning, little girl. You must have chased away my nightmares," she said as she stroked the purring animal.

Spectre rubbed her head against Aubrey's leg and meowed loudly.

"Are you telling me I should get up? I don't even know what time it is."

Aubrey wandered into the central hall and glanced at the grandfather clock, surprised to see it was already eleven. She'd slept for fifteen hours straight! Her stomach grumbled loudly, and she realized she was starving. She wondered what was available in the kitchen.

Rifling through the cabinets, she discovered the only food inside belonged to Spectre. She opened the refrigerator, frowning as she was greeted with nothing but empty shelves. Aubrey shouldn't have been surprised; after all, no one had lived there for six months besides the cat.

Of course, they had all known she was coming, so it would have been polite to supply at least a few staples. Maybe that's what Carlton had been hinting at when he'd asked if she needed anything. She had clearly missed that opportunity. Disappointed, she decided her plan for the day had to include purchasing food, since the can of soup she'd bought wouldn't last long. Aubrey grimaced at Spectre.

"I'll starve to death if I don't go into town. But the last thing I want is to revisit that horrible store. I suppose it can't be helped."

She meandered back to the foyer and spotted her suitcase sitting forlornly beside the front door. Although she didn't have many worldly possessions, she supposed it was time to unpack them. As she glanced furtively up the winding staircase, Aubrey's palms began to sweat. She hadn't forgotten the sight of the woman in the attic, or the strange footsteps she'd heard up there the night before.

Although Aubrey was afraid to explore the rest of Desolate Ridge, she knew she couldn't sleep on the couch forever. There were bedrooms up there, presumably with soft, cozy beds, and it was time to scout them out. It was daylight for the time being, and she intended to be finished before the sun went down again.

Taking a deep breath, Aubrey slowly ascended the stairs, Spectre trotting along behind her. The smooth wooden banister felt icy cool beneath her sweaty hand. She reached the landing and flipped on the light switch, illuminating the area. Sunlight was peeking in through the clerestory windows lining the top of the wall, yet she still felt the need to chase away the darkness of the space, either real or imagined.

One wall of the landing area boasted floor-to-ceiling bookshelves. Another glistening chandelier hung in the center of the room. A royal blue velvet chaise lounge rested against the other wall. If Aubrey hadn't been so much on edge, the space would have been a pleasant place to while away the hours.

Aubrey walked slowly to the balcony, peering over the edge of the banister, looking far below to the ground floor of the foyer. Suddenly she wanted to dance. She felt an intense urge to waltz, although she'd never done so in her life. Aubrey had the bizarre and unexplainable impression that being up so high made her feel as if she were flying. The landing area was at least sixteen feet high. Gripping the ledge, she leaned over a bit farther.

Without warning, her hands slipped from the railing, her body thudding against the balustrade.

With a gasp, she pulled herself to her feet, hands shaking, and caught her breath. If it weren't for the thin wooden spindles, Aubrey would have careened straight to the ground below.

Backing away from the balcony, she tried to gather her wits. Sinking onto the chaise lounge, she tried to make sense of what had happened. Without a doubt, Aubrey knew she hadn't slipped. She'd been pushed. She'd clearly felt the impression of flattened palms against her back, propelling her forward, trying to shove her over the edge and onto the gleaming hardwood floor below.

But that was ridiculous. She couldn't have been pushed. There was no one else in the house.

Aubrey reasoned that she must have lost her balance. There was no other logical explanation. Nevertheless, she wanted to get as far away from the railing as she could.

Trying to calm her nerves, she backed out of the room and continued on toward the hallway, noticing there were seven doors, six of which were open. Three well-appointed bedrooms sat to the right and three to the left. One of them, the master suite, was massive and boasted an opulent four-poster bed across from a large stone fireplace. There was an attached bathroom with a basin sink and a claw-foot bathtub.

Aubrey deposited her suitcase in that room, deciding she might as well take the best for herself.

Wandering back down the hallway, she approached the seventh door, which was closed. She ran her fingertips over the old polished wood of the door, feeling a strange longing to open it. Her hand gripped the crystal doorknob, but as she turned it, a woman's voice whispered, "I've been waiting for you."

She pulled her hand away from the knob as if it were on fire. The sapphire ring glinted and gleamed, squeezing her finger so tightly it nearly cut off her circulation. She tried to twist the band, but it wouldn't budge.

Aubrey spun around to see who had whispered in her ear. No one was there but Spectre, who meowed loudly, pacing back and forth quickly across the hardwood floor in an obvious state of agitation. Clearly something had also spooked the cat.

Aubrey's heart pounded. She'd heard the same voice the day before. It had seemed so real, but it couldn't have been. Her overactive imagination must have gotten the best of her. Shaking her head, she reached for the knob, turning it quickly before she could change her mind.

The heavy door creaked open on its hinges. Aubrey peered upward into the unknown, the wooden attic stairway curving around to an area that couldn't be seen from where she was standing. She needed to know what was up there. She'd told herself she was going to explore the entire house, and she intended to see it through.

Apprehensively, Aubrey stepped onto the bottom stair, the old wood moaning and sighing beneath the weight of her small body. With trepidation, she made her way up the stairs, telling herself it was only an attic. It was just another room. No matter how many times she said it, she remained unconvinced. A dark, ominous feeling permeated the area; a sinister ambience, invisible, but almost tangible.

She reached the top and looked around. Old furniture was covered in white sheets, haunting, standing like ghosts in the dimly lit room. Dust covered everything like a thin blanket of snow. Unlike the rest of the house, the attic was musty and unkempt. It was obvious that no one had been there in quite a while.

Secrets hung in the air. Aubrey felt the frantic tug of the room itself, clawing, trying desperately to hold on to its long-preserved enigma. The energy in the attic shifted as her footsteps disturbed the space, fluttering like desiccated leaves in a pile.

Large wooden trunks that appeared to be as old as the house itself stood as sentries, guarding the treasures of the past that lay inside. Gigantic wardrobes lined the walls. Aubrey wondered what mysteries she might unlock if she could work up the courage to look.

An old Bible, layered in at least twenty years' worth of dust, sat on a stand to her right. Curious, she opened the front cover. Her eyes widened when she saw a handwritten account of marriages, births, and deaths in the Ross family. She noted the slanted handwriting of the first entry. Squinting to read it, she managed to make out the names of Marshall Ross and Marie Stockton. It was dated 1819.

A creaking sound on the other side of the room caused her to jump. She slammed the Bible shut, trying to spot the source of the noise, but she saw nothing. Spectre looked pointedly at her, waiting to see what Aubrey would do next.

Deciding the Bible would be a good way to trace the crooked branches of her family tree, she grabbed the book, tucked it under her arm, and descended the attic stairs quickly. She turned off the light and slammed the door shut with a thud. If she never went up there again, it would be too soon.

CHAPTER TEN

Aubrey returned to the bedroom she'd claimed as her own and deposited the worn Bible on the bedside table. Unable to process anything at that moment, she decided she would peruse the information later. Still spooked from her experience in the attic, she took a few deep breaths and willed her heart to stop racing.

Once she'd calmed down, she changed her clothes, freshened up for the day, and headed downstairs. Spectre followed behind her like a shadow, seemingly glad to have a new companion. The feeling was mutual.

Aubrey had survived the task of exploring the rest of the house, so next on her list was procuring food.

"I don't want to go into town, Spectre, but there's no food here. Maybe someone would bring it to me if I asked, but I'm not asking," she said.

She fumbled through the kitchen cabinets, finally finding several sets of keys labeled "House," "Bentley," "Mercedes," "BMW," "Jaguar," and "Cadillac."

"Haven't these people ever heard of a Toyota? I suppose I'll take the BMW. See you in a bit, Spectre."

Aubrey grabbed the keys for both the house and the car, slipped her purse over her shoulder, and headed out the front door, locking it securely behind her. She didn't know where she was going, but Carlton had mentioned a garage.

She ambled to the side of the house, taking in the scenery as she went. The day was overcast, and the trees surrounding the estate had mostly lost their leaves. She spotted what appeared to be a rose garden in the distance. Crooked branches silhouetted an arch across the gray skyline. The grounds of Desolate Ridge were as immaculately cared for as the house. It was a breathtaking view.

As she rounded the corner, she saw a large building made from the same brick as the house. It had five bay doors, which more than likely concealed the five vehicles. Walking inside, she saw them lined up before her. They were shiny and well-maintained, not a speck of dust on them. She pushed the button on the key fob, and the lights flashed on a sleek BMW sedan. It was difficult to grasp that it all belonged to her.

"This is unbelievable," Aubrey whispered under her breath.

She opened the door of the car and slid behind the wheel. After pushing the garage door opener above the visor, the bay door slid open slowly. She started the vehicle, carefully backed out, and headed down the winding driveway. She wasn't sure if she remembered the route back into Rossdale, but she was going to give it a try.

Aubrey neared the end of the driveway and the gate glided open. She took a left out of the driveway and headed down the road. Desolate Ridge wasn't too far outside of the boundaries of Rossdale proper, so it wasn't long before she arrived.

She drove down Main Street, pulled into the parking lot of Lawson's General Store, and parked the car. Her stomach rumbled loudly, a reminder that she hadn't eaten since the previous day. She needed food and coffee, and she needed it quickly. Looking across the street, she noticed a small diner. The sign said Rebecca's Place.

She had worked in diners since she'd graduated from high school. They were comfortable and natural, far more familiar than driving a BMW or owning a mansion. She locked the car, sprinted across the street, and ducked inside the small restaurant.

The bell on the front door jingled as Aubrey entered, and everyone in the diner stopped eating and looked her way. Spoons and forks froze midair, and all conversation ceased. Curious glances mingled alongside outright hostility.

She was beginning to understand the citizens of Rossdale had no love for strangers, especially ones who happened to carry the Ross family name. She was unsure how they knew who she was, but clearly they did. It was a very small town, after all, a town that happened to be named after her family. Remaining anonymous was a pipe dream.

The awkward silence lingered a moment too long, and Aubrey was nearly ready to turn around and leave. Just then, a woman sporting a giant smile and exuding an air of kindness walked toward her. The woman's friendly face was like a life preserver being thrown Aubrey's way. She had long, straight, sandy-blonde hair, was tall and thin, and she was wearing a pink pin-striped apron.

"Hello there. Are you eating alone today?" Her wide smile immediately put Aubrey at ease, a phenomenon that rarely occurred.

"Yes, I'm always alone," Aubrey answered with the slightest smirk.

"Come this way. I'll put you at my favorite table, the one back there in the corner, away from all of the prying eyes," the woman answered with a grin and a wink of understanding.

"Thank you. I appreciate it. I despise being in a fishbowl," Aubrey replied.

Aubrey slid into the corner booth, and the woman handed her a menu.

"My name is Rebecca, and I'm the owner, by the way."

"My name is Aubrey. Aubrey Ross."

Aubrey waited for the woman to flinch when she revealed her last name was Ross. She expected Rebecca's warmth to turn frigid. She suspected the woman might even ask her to leave. But Rebecca did none of those things. She just continued to smile kindly.

"It's nice to meet you, Aubrey. I'll give you a minute to look over the menu, and then I'll stop back. I recommend the french toast. I promise you; it's the best thing you'll eat today."

"Thanks for the suggestion, Rebecca. I think I'll forgo

looking at the menu and just order the french toast, then. I'm starving."

"I'll go tell the cook, who happens to be my husband, Jake. I'll bring you some coffee too. You look like you need some," she laughed.

"Is it that obvious?"

"I know people, and you have the look of a girl who could use a coffee. I'll be right back."

Rebecca pivoted on her heel and walked toward the kitchen. She called out the order, grabbed the coffeepot, and headed back to Aubrey's table. She filled a large mug with the steaming liquid and scooted it toward Aubrey, who accepted the offering gratefully. She inhaled the scent, took a sip, and sighed with contentment. It was exactly what she needed.

"That's delicious. I'm from Seattle, and I'm a bit of a coffee snob, so I know a good cup when I taste one," Aubrey said between sips.

"You're from Seattle, huh? Rossdale must be a big change for you," Rebecca replied as she slid into the booth and sat across from Aubrey.

"Yeah, just a bit. I've never lived anywhere but there, so I don't have a lot to compare it to, but Rossdale is a whole different world."

"I'm sure it is."

"And I'm pretty sure I don't quite fit in." Aubrey glanced around the room. "Then again, I've never really fit anywhere, so I'm used to it."

"That's something a person should never get used to,"

Rebecca said kindly.

Aubrey wasn't sure how to respond. Conversations that burrowed beneath surface matters usually made her nervous. She'd so rarely encountered genuine kindness and caring in her life that it was a completely foreign concept. Yet something about Rebecca calmed her. Although it was strange, she liked the woman. Aubrey wasn't a conversationalist, but Rebecca made her want to try.

"Have you always lived in Rossdale, Rebecca?"

"Oh, yes. Both sides of my family have been in this town for a couple hundred years. I've never lived anywhere else," Rebecca replied with a laugh.

"Your whole family lives here?"

Aubrey couldn't imagine having a family. She couldn't fathom being connected to another person.

"Yep. My parents and grandparents live just down the road from me and Jake. We got married a couple of years ago and decided we wanted to be close by when we have our own kids. My brother, Hank, lives just a few miles away too. He's the sheriff in town," Rebecca explained.

"The sheriff is your brother?"

Aubrey thought back to the previous night. She hadn't exactly been kind to him.

"Hank's a pretty great guy, even though we fight like cats and dogs most of the time." Rebecca giggled.

"Yeah, I actually met the sheriff last night," Aubrey began.

"Oh really?"

"He stopped by the house because all the lights were on.

Apparently wasting electricity is a crime around here."

"Well, Desolate Ridge has been empty for months. Hank was probably just making sure it wasn't an intruder or something," Rebecca told her.

"I never thought of that," Aubrey admitted. "I suppose I was on edge, being in a strange house and all."

"That makes sense. Being inside that house would put anyone on edge," Rebecca said with a raised eyebrow.

The woman seemed to regret her words as soon as she said them. Her eyes grew wide, and her hand flew up to cover her mouth.

"Oh, Aubrey, I'm so sorry. That was rude. I shouldn't have said that about your family's house. It's just that... well... Desolate Ridge has always been a bit of an urban legend around here."

"An urban legend?"

"Yes. People are basically terrified of the place."

Aubrey shook her head. "I don't really understand any of this. Until a few days ago, I had never even heard of Desolate Ridge, or Rossdale."

"You didn't know about your family's house?"

"Everything has been thrown into my lap, and no one has told me anything. I know nothing about that house or the Ross family. I always thought being an orphan was tough, but I'm beginning to believe that may have been the easy part," Aubrey explained.

"What do you mean? You didn't know your family?"

Instinctively, Rebecca reached across the table and placed her hand over Aubrey's. Under any other circumstances,

Aubrey would have flinched at the touch of a stranger. She couldn't figure out what it was about the other woman that made her feel so comfortable, but Rebecca had an innate, genuine kindness that drew Aubrey in.

"It's such a long story, Rebecca, and I'm sure you don't want to hear the sordid details of my miserable life." Aubrey shrugged, unsure of what else to say.

A bell rang in the kitchen, signaling her food was ready.

"I'll go grab your order. Be right back," Rebecca said as she rose from the table.

Rebecca returned promptly with a plate of the most delectable-looking french toast Aubrey had ever seen.

"I'm going to leave you alone so you can eat your meal in peace, but I just want you to know I'm really glad to meet you. I can't imagine what it must be like, being in a new town, in a strange house, and searching for answers," Rebecca said.

"Thank you. That's really nice of you. I'm not... used to that sort of thing."

"What sort of thing?"

"Kindness."

A look of deep sorrow passed over Rebecca's face. She paused a moment, then continued. "Are you free the day after tomorrow, Aubrey?"

"Free? For what?"

"My family is coming to my house for dinner, just like they do every Sunday, and I'd really like it if you'd join us."

"You want me to join you and your family for dinner? You don't even know me."

"Yes. It seems like you haven't received a decent welcome to Rossdale, and I'd like to fix that."

"Oh, no, I really couldn't do that. I don't want to be a bother, or an intruder," Aubrey answered with a shake of her head.

"It's no bother at all, and my parents would love to meet you. My grandparents will be there too. They've lived in Rossdale forever. Maybe they can answer some of your questions about your family."

Rebecca's words stopped Aubrey in her tracks. She wanted information, and Rebecca was offering that possibility.

"All right. That would actually be helpful. As long as you're sure no one will mind," Aubrey replied.

"I have just officially made you my new friend, which in my mind qualifies you as family, so no one will mind you being there. In fact, we'll expect it."

Rebecca winked and smiled widely before leaving Aubrey alone to finish her meal. She gobbled up the french toast, drank another cup of coffee, and paid her bill. Rebecca handed her a slip of paper with her address scribbled on it, then waved goodbye.

Aubrey headed across the street to Lawson's General Store, where she filled a cart with food staples, as well as a few splurge items she wouldn't ordinarily purchase. It was the first time in her life that she carried her groceries to the checkout counter without a second thought about how much everything would cost. Cammie Lawson was working at the register once again, and she gave Aubrey a curious glance but said nothing. Aubrey simply smiled politely, not wanting to initiate a conversation with the girl.

She loaded her groceries into the car and headed back toward Desolate Ridge. She hadn't wanted to make the trip into Rossdale, but the experience wasn't at all what she'd expected. Somehow, against her better judgment, she'd made a friend. It was a first.

Aubrey pulled up to the gate of Desolate Ridge and watched it slide open, then traversed the winding driveway through the thicket of trees. As the house came into view, she paused for a moment to take it all in. Knowing it belonged to her still felt surreal, but she was gradually accepting the reality.

As Aubrey started to pull the car into the garage, she glanced toward the attic window. The woman in the white gown with the cascading hair was up there once again.

CHAPTER ELEVEN

Desolate Ridge
1841

Byron Ross watched as his wife, Emilia, and their son, George, frolicked through the lush, rolling yard of Desolate Ridge. Emilia gathered her skirt and petticoat as she flounced across the grass in an effort to make their young son laugh. The pearl necklace Byron had given her on their wedding day rested on her dainty neck. A frilly linen cap adorned her head, but Emilia's golden spaniel curls bounced delightfully free of the restraints. A thin shawl covered her delicate shoulders. Byron thought his wife was as lovely as a porcelain doll.

George, just two years old, grinned widely at his mother. The lad noticed his father gazing at them through the window. He giggled, waving his chubby hands and motioning for Byron to join them. The young boy created a handsome picture in his tunic suit. A flat cap covered his chestnut waves, which he'd inherited from his ancestors. The proud father loved his son more than life itself.

Byron watched as Emilia danced across the lawn. He believed having a beautiful wife was a double-edged sword. Emilia Duncan had been the belle of every ball, the most desired debutante in the county. Byron had set his sights on her. He had wanted her, and she had chosen him from among all of her suitors.

He should have felt a sense of pride in being the one to win her heart. Most men would have been happy about such a conquest. The problem was, no matter how hard he tried, Byron Ross wasn't like most men. He tried to be, but his true nature had become increasingly difficult to conceal.

His father, Marshall, had always excused Byron's strange behavior; after all, it seemed to run in the Ross family. Byron had known from a young age that there was something wrong with him, just as he'd always known there was something wrong with his father.

Byron wasn't like other boys, but he didn't know why. Perhaps it had been precipitated by the disappearance of his mother, Marie, when he was just an infant. Byron was told that one day his mother simply vanished, leaving him behind.

There had been rumors of impropriety and scandal surrounding the strange circumstances in the disappearance of Marie Ross, but no one knew what really happened. Or if they did, the facts had been buried long ago.

He didn't understand the source of his deranged thoughts, and yet they had always been there, causing his blood to boil just a little too savagely. Byron couldn't contain the heat, and the anger would flow like hot lava, bubbling right through his skin. He could always see it coming, yet he was powerless to stop it.

Byron also had visions, terrible images of destructive behaviors he felt compelled to execute. He was hounded by voices warning him that horrible things would come to pass if he didn't obey the compulsions. It was maddening, exhausting, and all too much to bear.

When Byron was younger, he'd been able to quiet the voices if he tried hard enough. He'd figured out ways to mute the whisperings in his brain. He'd ignored the visions, and sometimes, they went away completely. But since the birth of his son, they seemed to be getting worse, coming more frequently and gaining in momentum.

Byron didn't know if he could control the impulses much longer. Rather, they seemed to have increasing control over him. Something told him the voices wouldn't be silent until he obeyed their commands.

Byron's eyes settled once again on his young wife and son. Lately the voices had been telling him he shouldn't have a wife at all. The whispers in his brain hinted that sooner or later, Emilia, his lovely, pure, gentle angel, would begin to understand the monster that lived inside her husband. When that happened, everything would be ripped from his grasp. Emilia would take George away and leave Byron behind.

If Emilia really knew the man she was married to, she would run as fast and as far as she could.

Byron Ross knew he wouldn't survive the loss of his son.

If that happened, it would surely be the end of him. There was only one answer—in order to keep Emilia from taking his son, he had to get rid of her.

There were many ways to do it. If he staged the event correctly, no one would suspect a thing. The voices had told him the way it should happen. All he had to do was go along with the plan. He would miss his wife, but he would think about that later.

The couple loved to dance together, and Emilia's favorite spot to waltz was on the second-floor landing of Desolate Ridge. She loved to look at the world below her as she and her husband twirled across the room, saying the height made her feel as if she were flying.

The voices told Byron that solving his problem would be easy. All he had to do was dance with his wife. When their bodies moved close to the railing, and he pushed her, just a little, he could set her free. She would never have to stop loving him. She would never have to discover the darkness that lived inside him. She would never be able to take George away.

Byron wanted his beautiful Emilia to fly forever as the angel she was. Maybe then the voices would stop.

CHAPTER TWELVE

The next day, Aubrey had just finished creating a to-do list when she heard the crunching of tires in the driveway. Spooked by the image of the woman in the attic, she'd barely been able to sleep the previous night. Instead, she'd whiled away the seemingly endless hours of darkness by writing down questions she needed answered. She'd also put together a list of tasks to be completed before she could sell the house. The sooner she could get the money from Desolate Ridge and be on her way, the better.

She saw two men and a woman get out of the car in the driveway. She assumed they must be Mr. and Mrs. Bonaventure, and their son, Anson. Carlton had mentioned the couple and their son were the caretakers who came every day to work on household tasks. They hadn't shown up the day before, but Aubrey guessed they were giving her time to get settled. She watched through the window as the trio approached the front door.

Mr. Bonaventure was a frowning, sturdy-looking man

who appeared to be in his midsixties. He had salt-and-pepper hair and barely a wrinkle on his face. It was obvious he performed manual labor for a living, as he seemed strong and stout.

Mrs. Bonaventure appeared to be about the same age as her husband. She was pleasantly plump, wore a comfortable smile, and had the look of a woman who was used to being in charge. Her face was pretty, and Aubrey imagined she'd been quite a beauty in her younger years.

Their son, Anson, was a handsome, dark-eyed, raven-haired man with broad shoulders, large arms, and a trim physique. His face was youthful, even though she imagined he must be in his forties. He glanced around anxiously, as if he would rather be anywhere but there.

Aubrey heard the doorbell ring, and she was surprised, having assumed the caretakers had a key and would therefore come right in. She decided they must be respecting her privacy, waiting for her to answer the door.

Aubrey rolled her eyes and took a deep breath. She hated meeting people. She hoped they wouldn't expect small talk, because conversation didn't interest her in the least.

She opened the door and tried to smile, but it came across as more of a smirk.

"You must be the caretakers," she said.

"We are the Bonaventures. It is so nice to meet you, dear. We've been excited ever since Mr. Wayfair told us you were coming." Mrs. Bonaventure gushed as she pulled Aubrey into a hug.

She wasn't sure how to respond. Physical affection made

her uncomfortable. She didn't like to be touched. Caught off guard, she allowed herself to be engulfed in the other woman's arms, although she didn't return the gesture. She stood there stiffly, waiting for it to end.

"Oh, I'm sorry. You'll have to forgive me. I'm a hugger. I forget not everyone feels the same," Mrs. Bonaventure explained as she released Aubrey. "My name is Coral, this is my husband, Michael, and that's our son, Anson."

"It's nice to meet you," Aubrey answered quietly.

Mr. Bonaventure scowled and nodded slightly before disappearing into the other room. He seemed to be a man of few words. His wife didn't suffer from the same affliction as her husband. She prattled on without taking a breath, and Aubrey tuned out the chatter somewhere after the second sentence. Instead, her focus rested on their son, Anson.

He hadn't spoken, but he also hadn't left the room. He stood behind his mother, his hands stuffed in his pockets, trying to disguise the fact that he was staring back at Aubrey. She pretended to listen to Mrs. Bonaventure's ramblings, but she was as riveted on Anson as he was on her.

Something about the man set her on high alert, although she couldn't quite put her finger on the reason why. Aubrey had the unsettling sensation of a connection, as if she knew Anson from somewhere, although that was impossible.

Nevertheless, when she looked at him, she was flooded with sadness, longing, and an unexplainable feeling of wistfulness. His eyes locked onto hers, and she was overwhelmed by a familiarity she didn't understand.

"You look just like her," the man muttered quietly.

"Just like who?" Aubrey asked.

"Anna."

Mrs. Bonaventure threw a sideways glance at her son. He caught his mother's gaze and seemed to instantly regret the fact that he'd broken his silence. Without another word, he turned on his heels and headed out the front door.

"He knew my mother? Did you know her too?" Aubrey hoped Mrs. Bonaventure, who clearly enjoyed talking, would be a great source of information.

"Of course we knew Anna. I've worked for the Ross family since I was a young girl. So has Mr. Bonaventure."

"Oh, good. Maybe you can help me, then."

"Help you with what, dear?"

"Answer some questions," Aubrey replied.

"What questions might that be?"

"Why did my mother leave home?"

"Well now… I guess I… can't answer that. She had some… trouble… with your grandparents," the woman stammered by way of explanation.

"What kind of trouble?"

"Your grandparents had high and clear expectations. Your mother had her own opinions, and a sadness that hovered over her wherever she went. And then there was… well, like I said, I don't really know."

Aubrey was aware that the woman knew far more than she said. Mrs. Bonaventure had almost said something else, yet for some unknown reason, she'd censored herself.

Mrs. Bonaventure smiled and headed upstairs without another word. Aubrey heard her banging around in the bedroom above. The conversation, which had ended abruptly, was over.

Mrs. Bonaventure's love of chatter apparently didn't extend to matters of the Ross family. In fact, no one in Rossdale seemed inclined to speak of them.

Aubrey wandered into the kitchen and spotted Anson in the backyard with a weed eater. He worked efficiently and effortlessly. She watched the way he moved, gracefully, powerfully, like an athlete. He made Aubrey uncomfortable and curious at the same time. She wanted to run away from him, and yet she felt compelled to know more about the man.

His mother wasn't forthcoming with information, but if she could get to know Anson, perhaps he would be.

She heard heavy footsteps coming down the stairway, and Mrs. Bonaventure entered the kitchen.

"He's a hard worker, that son of mine," she said quietly, almost as if she were talking to herself.

"Yes, it looks like it," Aubrey agreed as she continued to stare at him.

"Since you're officially in control of the house, is there anything specific you would like us to do when we come?"

Her words caused Aubrey to look away from the window.

"I've made a list. I'll be selling the house soon, and there are a few things I'd like to have completed before I put it on the market," Aubrey answered matter-of-factly.

"You're selling Desolate Ridge? But it's been in your family for two hundred years!"

The shock on the woman's face was obvious.

"Yes, I understand that. But I don't want it, and it's mine to sell. I have no need for it," Aubrey replied curtly. "I left the list on the counter."

Ignoring the surprised look on Mrs. Bonaventure's face, she walked across the kitchen to where she'd left the note on the countertop.

It wasn't there.

"Did you take it already?"

"Take what, dear?"

"The to-do list I made. It was on the counter when I answered the door, and it's not there now," Aubrey replied irritably.

"I haven't seen a list. I just came in here a second ago," she answered.

"That doesn't make sense. It was just there...."

Aubrey searched the area where she'd left the note. She even got on her hands and knees and looked on the floor beneath the counter. As she stood to her feet, she glanced inside the trash can. It was empty, except for a single wad of paper.

Aubrey reached inside the bin and pulled it out, recognizing it immediately. It was the list she'd made, which had been crumpled into a ball and thrown away.

"Why was this in the trash can?" she questioned Mrs. Bonaventure.

"Well, I wouldn't know, dear. No one has been in here but you."

"But that doesn't make any sense. I didn't throw it away. I left it on the counter when I answered the door."

Nothing about Desolate Ridge was logical. Aubrey was beginning to believe she had somehow crossed over an invisible threshold between madness and sanity. She'd teetered on the border her entire life; perhaps she'd finally made the final decisive leap. The crumpled paper was just another addition to the list of odd experiences since she'd arrived.

"I don't understand. I know I left this list on the counter," Aubrey insisted as she held the paper in her hand.

"I wouldn't worry about it, dear. Some things around here just can't be explained," Mrs. Bonaventure answered cryptically.

"I don't believe that. There's a logical explanation for everything."

"Of course there is. I'm going to go dust the parlor," the older woman replied with a nod.

Alone with her thoughts, Aubrey tried to make sense of things. No one had been in the kitchen besides her, and she hadn't thrown the list into the trash can. Not only had it been thrown away, it had been deliberately crumpled into a wad, as if someone were trying to make a point.

Tapping her fingertips on the counter in agitation, Aubrey glanced out the kitchen window and saw Anson trimming a bush. She decided to ask him if he'd seen anyone in the house.

As she angled her body toward the far side of the lawn, her eye caught sight of the rose garden she'd noticed the day before. Suddenly, she needed to see it, feeling that doing so was the most vital requirement of her life.

She turned and walked in the opposite direction of where she'd intended to go. She made a beeline toward the garden, as if she had no choice in the matter. Her body felt directed and tugged by forces beyond her control.

The closer she came to the arbor, the heavier her steps grew. Aubrey trudged slowly through the grass, and as she walked, she began to cry. The tears fell slowly at first, but soon they trailed down her cheeks like a waterfall cascading over a precipice. She didn't know why she was crying, yet she couldn't stop.

She approached the trellis, hanging heavily with tangling, crawling roses. The tears continued to fall as if there were an endless supply. Aubrey could have cried forever and it wouldn't have been long enough to purge the woe that seeped into her very core. The deep, all-consuming sadness engulfed her, a despondent mournfulness, like her heart had been irreparably shattered.

Sobs racked Aubrey's body as she opened the wooden gate that led to the garden. She stepped inside the entrance and nearly collapsed onto a wrought iron bench. The beauty of the blooming roses was overshadowed by an oppressive feeling of melancholy. It hung in the air like a thick, dense fog.

Aubrey couldn't understand why she'd felt obliged to visit the garden. She didn't know why she'd been overcome with anguish. Like most things at Desolate Ridge, it made no sense.

As she glanced helplessly around the secluded garden, her breath caught in her throat. Scattered across the ground, like flowers tossed into the wind, were six small, flat grave markers. In shock, she glanced at the names and dates. All six read "Baby Boy Ross" and listed only the death dates.

Aubrey wiped her eyes as understanding dawned—the children had died before they'd ever had the chance to live.

CHAPTER THIRTEEN

Desolate Ridge
1866

George Ross wandered through the rose garden alone. Pulling the bottle of laudanum from his breast pocket, he placed several drops on his tongue, then slumped onto the wrought iron bench and closed his eyes, willing the sweet euphoria of the elixir to be speedy. His use of the laudanum had increased substantially, but he couldn't function without it. He didn't want to feel anything. It was all too much.

He glanced around the garden, wiping the tears from his eyes as he looked at the six small headstones. He didn't know why he tortured himself by visiting, yet he did. The hidden cemetery seemed a fitting place for what he intended to do.

He'd received word only an hour earlier that Anne, his wife, had killed herself in the asylum. She'd been there only a few months, but it had apparently been too long.

George didn't want to send his wife away, but he could barely take care of himself, let alone Anne or their one-year-old son, Peter.

The six headstones swam before his eyes, mocking his pain. Every pregnancy had sent George and Anne deeper into despair. By the time Peter finally came along, Anne was lost in an abyss of grief and couldn't find her way out. George was no better, numbing his pain with laudanum just to survive.

He had no explanation for the depression that had haunted him since boyhood. The tragic death of his mother, Emilia, was perhaps part of the reason. He hadn't seen her fall from the second-story landing of their home, but he'd lived with the terrible ramifications of the loss.

George's father, Byron, had never been the same after the death of his wife. He'd shuffled through the halls of Desolate Ridge day after day, a skeleton of a man, raving about "the voices." No one understood what he was talking about. The doctors declared Byron mad, irrevocably broken, but harmless. So they'd medicated George's ailing father, allowing him to stay at Desolate Ridge until he'd finally taken his own life.

Everyone whispered about the horrible accident that had killed Emilia Ross, but George believed it had killed them all in some ways. George had lost his mother in the accident, and his father as a result of it. A dark cloud of gloom had followed him throughout his life.

When George Ross met the lovely Anne Ashbridge, he had hoped she might bring him some light. Unfortunately, he quickly discovered that Anne shared his predisposition for sadness. They tried to chase away the shadows together, feeling as if their love could conquer the melancholy they shared, living so close to the surface.

They married, and Anne was soon with child. The couple believed the birth of their baby would finally bring them some joy. But it wasn't to be. One miscarriage turned into five. With each loss Anne suffered, the darkness crept closer. After losing her sixth child, Anne was unable to feel anything but despair. Then she became pregnant once again.

Throughout her pregnancy with Peter, Anne barely acknowledged the fact that she was expecting. Even as she passed all the milestones she'd never reached with the other pregnancies, she refused to accept that she would finally be a mother. She'd had too many crushing disappointments; she was no longer capable of hope.

When Peter was born, Anne refused to hold him. Soon after, she wouldn't get out of bed. She kept the curtains in her room drawn all day, refusing to allow even a sliver of light to enter. The doctors finally institutionalized Anne, and George let them. He had failed his family.

George Ross withdrew inside himself, believing the poison of his gloom had infected those he loved. Everything was his fault. His despair was too strong to allow anything near him to flourish. His depression had been too potent for the children in his wife's womb to survive.

He had driven Anne to insanity, and she'd killed herself in the asylum. He knew his toxicity would consume young Peter if he allowed it to. The only way to ensure that didn't happen was to stay away from his son.

Desperately, George dropped to his knees as the sobs racked his body. He reached one tentative hand toward the gravestone closest to him, caressing the etched lettering. The sadness was more than he could stand. It was a monster on his back, pushing, shoving him down until he could no longer rise. He collapsed onto the hard ground, his body lying prostrate beside the shrine to his children.

His hands trembled as he once again reached for the laudanum bottle in his breast pocket. He'd already taken far too much, yet the darkness lingered. The numbness that used to embrace him with each drop refused to come near. The blissful oblivion of the drug had abandoned him, just as his parents had. Ironically, he was perpetuating the legacy of desertion with his own son. But he was too weak to care.

He tipped the laudanum bottle on end, draining its entire contents into his mouth. Soon it would all be over. He had tried to fight the darkness, but it had won.

CHAPTER FOURTEEN

Aubrey had fallen asleep with the light on, as always. Before bed, she'd finally worked up the courage to peruse the Ross family Bible. As she'd read over the births, deaths, and marriages, she was struck with a revelation—the women in her family all died very young.

With the exception of her grandmother, Elizabeth, every woman who had married into the Ross family was Aubrey's age or younger when she passed away. Why did these women, seemingly youthful and vibrant, die by the age of twenty-five? How had they died? Who was the mother of the babies in the rose garden? The death dates on their headstones spanned less than a three-year period, so Aubrey assumed one mother had grieved the loss of them all. Also eerie was the fact that each generation of the Ross family produced a single living child, always a male—except for Aubrey and her mother.

Each new discovery was stranger and more unsettling than the last. There must have been a reason for everything.

Aubrey needed to know.

She tossed and turned in the mammoth four-poster bed. Her sleep patterns had been abnormal since arriving at Desolate Ridge, and the restlessness was beginning to catch up with her. The line between real and imaginary had become so blurred she could barely tell the difference anymore.

Spectre hissed, startling Aubrey. She shot up in bed, chills erupting on every inch of her skin. The hair on her arms rose on end, and the back of her neck prickled. Her eye began to twitch as she heard the unsettling sound of a woman crying. It wasn't a soft whimpering but was instead a keening wail.

Her heart pounded in her chest as she deliberated about what to do. The sound was too loud to ignore, yet the thought of leaving the safety of her bed was unconscionable.

Her racing pulse throbbed in her finger as the sapphire ring squeezed tightly, gripping like a vise. The woman's weeping continued, growing in volume. Aubrey twisted the ring, the blue of the stone glowing hauntingly. Or was that just her imagination?

It seemed that since she'd slipped the piece of jewelry onto her finger, nothing had been normal. Aubrey tugged, trying to remove the ring, but her effort was in vain. The jewelry wouldn't budge. In fact, it seemed to be growing tighter by the moment.

The woman's crying intensified. Aubrey had no choice but to investigate.

She crept from the master bedroom and made her way

into the hall. As she neared the doorway leading upstairs to the attic, the noise level increased. She'd only been in the attic once, and she had no desire to do so again, especially in the middle of the night. But she had to find out what was going on.

Someone was up there.

Aubrey needed a flashlight, but she remembered it was in the kitchen. She padded softly down the winding staircase to retrieve it. As she neared the bottom of the stairs, she began to cough. The distinct smell of smoke trailed into her nostrils, choking her with its pungency. Something was on fire!

She ran toward the odor, choking and sputtering as she went. The scorching smell was coming from the sitting room. Aubrey's brain refused to work quickly. She should have dialed 911, but the image of Sheriff Metzger came to mind instead.

She remembered feeling compelled to program his number into her phone the night he'd handed her his card. She didn't know why she'd done so, as she'd had no intention of ever using it. Rather than question it, she simply dialed.

"This is Aubrey Ross. There's a fire," she screamed into the phone when he picked up.

She reached the sitting room and was nearly knocked over by the scorching heat. Flames licked and danced, burning with fervor. The entire room was engulfed in the blaze. She covered her mouth and nose with her nightgown, but the all-consuming firestorm was too much. She tried to take shallow breaths, but the angry flames released a sulfurous odor.

Aubrey grew dizzy, and the room began to spin before her eyes. *Why has he done this to us?* The phrase, which made no sense, grew louder in her muddled brain. She began to scream in an effort to drown out the words, but they continued to swim in her mind. *Why has he done this to us?*

The phone dropped to the floor. Her eyes watered as she continued to choke. She tried to open the sitting room door, but it had closed behind her. She banged on the unyielding door, twisting the knob frantically, but it was no use. She was locked inside.

Why has he done this to us?

She just needed to get to the window. If she could pry it open, she would be safe.

Get to the window!

It was her last thought before she passed out.

CHAPTER FIFTEEN

Desolate Ridge
1897

Peter Ross paced back and forth across the hardwood floor of his study. His rage burned as hot as an inferno. His wife had taken things too far. She had crossed the line. She had embarrassed him.

She had to be stopped.

He lit his cigar and sighed deeply. A plume of smoke swirled in the air. When he'd married Catherine Sykes, he'd had suspicions that the woman would be unfaithful. A woman like her was too beautiful, too perfect to ever be satisfied with only one man. Stupidly, he'd believed his love could change her. He'd been wrong.

Like the shifting of the tides, Peter's anger ebbed, giving way to sadness. He slumped into the chair behind his desk and buried his face in his hands. His body shook with sobs that he couldn't contain. His moods were mercurial, swinging back and forth like the pendulum on the grandfather clock in the hallway, vacillating from outrage to anguish in a matter of seconds. He couldn't control them, and he was exhausted from trying.

Catherine had to be stopped.

As he'd done his whole life, he wished he could talk to his parents. But that was impossible since he'd never known them. His mother, Anne, had died when he was just one year old, immediately followed by his father, George. No one ever said how they died. The graves of his six brothers lined the ground inside the rose garden. He'd found them when he was a young boy. He was told they had all died before birth but was given nothing more.

Peter often wondered if his parents died from sadness, but all questions about his family went unanswered. Instead of being raised by loving parents, surrounded by siblings, he had been raised alone by a maid and a butler. His physical needs were met, but his emotional needs were neglected.

He'd grown up in boarding schools, and by the time he'd returned to claim his place at Desolate Ridge, his swiftly shifting, unpredictable moods were out of control. Terrified and confused, he'd done his best to manage alone. For a while he was successful, but the personality changes had become impossible to ignore.

Catherine had begged him to get help, arguing their two-year-old son, Clarence, needed a father he could look up to. His wife's pleas did nothing but anger him. Catherine believed herself to be superior. She looked down on him, laughed at him behind his back. He knew it. That's exactly what he'd seen earlier that day.

She had to be stopped.

Peter knew his wife couldn't be trusted. No one as beautiful as Catherine could be faithful. He'd come upon them in the backyard, his wife and the gardener, laughing at some shared secret. Catherine swore she was only being kind, assured her angry husband she was simply telling the gardener how to prune the rose garden.

He didn't believe her. He knew there was more to it. Why had their laughter stopped as soon as they'd seen him? Because Peter was the object of their joke. They were laughing at him. Catherine told her irrational husband his jealousy was unfounded. She begged Peter to believe she only loved him. She and their son, Clarence, adored him. No matter how much she protested, Peter knew she was lying.

He closed his eyes and pictured his wife, her lovely corkscrew copper curls bouncing as she laughed. Her pale, perfect skin was the canvas for the bluest eyes he had ever seen. She pretended to be sweet and innocent, but he knew better. She pretended to be faithful, but she wasn't. She was a liar. She had bewitched him. She was deceitful, and she'd fooled him into marrying her.

She had to be stopped.

Peter heard Catherine laughing in the sitting room. She and Clarence were playing a game together. His son laughed just like his mother. He was sure they were both mocking him. He knew it. If he didn't do something, Clarence would grow up to be a liar, just like his mother.

She had to be stopped.

Peter's sadness subsided and his rage burned hot once again. Without a second thought, he stalked toward the sitting room. The fire was already lit in the fireplace; all he had to do was make it spread. He walked through the door and sat on the chair next to the hearth, all the while watching his wife and son as they played. They barely acknowledged him as he entered the room.

She had to be stopped.

They were distracted. He slowly opened the grate that covered the flames, then grabbed the throw pillow that was positioned on the chair beside him. He leaned forward and lit the edge of the pillow on fire. The lace began to curl as the flames took hold.

He hurled the pillow across the room, and it landed below the drapes covering the large window. Before long, the material was set ablaze. Within seconds, that side of the room was burning.

He grabbed the blanket that was next to him, set it on fire, and threw it toward the opposite side. Within seconds, the sitting room was engulfed in flames. Without even a backward glance, Peter left the room, locking the door tightly behind him.

She had to be stopped.

He refused to listen to the sound of his young son crying in fear. He ignored the ear-piercing screams of his wife, begging him for help. He blocked out the sound of glass shattering behind the barred door. He tuned everything out.

Catherine had left him no choice. He had to do it. She had laughed at him. She had been unfaithful. She was a liar. She had to be stopped.

CHAPTER SIXTEEN

"Aubrey, wake up. It's Hank Metzger. Can you hear me?"

A deep voice began to permeate the fog as Aubrey slowly opened her eyes. She wasn't sure if she was awake or dreaming. Hank's worried face loomed over hers. He was kneeling beside her, his warm hand on her ice-cold wrist. He was taking her pulse.

"What happened?"

Confusion swam in her brain. She was on the floor of the sitting room but had no idea why. The last thing she remembered was being awakened by the sound of crying in the attic.

"Aubrey, you called me and said there was a fire," Hank answered slowly.

Aubrey worked hard to remember, and suddenly it all came crashing back. She recalled the smell of smoke, the crackling, blistering flames, and her inability to take a breath. She'd been trapped in the sitting room, locked in tightly. All she'd wanted to do was get out of the room, to open the window, but she couldn't.

"There was a fire. This entire room was on fire."

She sat up quickly and looked around. Everything was perfectly intact. There wasn't a single trace of a flame. Nothing was burned, and there wasn't a speck of smoke damage. The sitting room looked exactly as it always had. Aubrey felt panic rise in her chest as she realized there was no explanation for what she'd experienced.

"I don't understand. I swear to you this room was on fire."

"Just take a few breaths, Aubrey."

"It doesn't make sense. I was locked inside and couldn't get out."

Aubrey's breath came faster. She was hyperventilating. Nothing made sense. She was going crazy. The house was driving her mad.

"I'm crazy. I'm going crazy."

"Aubrey, listen to me. You're safe. Look at me and breathe with me," Hank replied calmly.

Aubrey's eyes bored into the sheriff's. She reached out and grabbed his hands, clinging to him with all her might. She had to find a way to anchor herself in this world before she was sucked into the next. She worked to match her breath with his, and before long, her gasps gave way to normal respiration.

"There you go. Now you're coming back."

Hank spoke quietly, in slow, soothing tones. He rhythmically traced his thumbs across the tops of Aubrey's hands while she clutched his tightly. She felt the terror melt and the calmness begin to settle inside. Slowly, her heart rate returned to normal.

"I'm... I'm sorry. I don't... understand... what happened," she managed.

"I don't know either, Aubrey, but something clearly did."

"You must think I've lost my mind."

"Why don't we go sit down, and you can try to remember."

Hank helped her to her feet and led her out of the sitting room, down the hall, and into the parlor, hoping the change of scenery might soothe her and jog her memory. She shivered violently. Hank realized it was from shock, so he grabbed a velvet throw blanket and draped it around Aubrey's trembling shoulders.

"There you go. Just take a few minutes and try to gather your thoughts," he soothed.

Aubrey was embarrassed. She wasn't used to asking for help, yet she'd called Hank in hysterical desperation. To make the situation worse, it had all been for no reason. There wasn't a fire. She'd imagined the entire thing. Hank probably thought she had lost her mind. And he might be right.

"Look, I'm sorry to have bothered you, Sheriff Metzger, but you can go now."

She stood quickly, squared her shoulders, and lifted her chin. Somehow she had to find a way to regain her dignity. She couldn't have the town sheriff thinking she was a lunatic, even if she was.

"It's really no bother at all. Please sit down, Aubrey.

I'd like to help you get to the bottom of this." Hank gestured toward the couch. Reluctantly Aubrey took a seat.

"You really don't have to stay. It was probably just a bad dream."

"I don't think it was a dream."

"You don't?"

"No, I don't," he answered matter-of-factly.

"Then you probably think I'm crazy," she retorted.

"I don't think you're crazy. I think something happened here tonight. I don't think it was a dream, and I don't think it was in your head."

Aubrey scrutinized Hank's face, looking for any indication he was lying. She hated to be pitied, and there was nothing worse than being patronized. She knew how to read people, having done it her whole life. She could spot a liar from a mile away. But when she looked at Hank, all she could see was genuine sincerity. It was the same experience she'd had with his sister, Rebecca.

"Look, the problem is I don't know what happened. Nothing has made sense to me since the minute I inherited this place," Aubrey admitted.

"Tell me what you remember tonight. Let's start there," Hank encouraged.

"Before I went to sleep, I was reading over the names in the front of this old family Bible I found in the attic," Aubrey started.

"I'll bet that made for some interesting bedtime reading," he quipped.

"You have no idea."

"What did you find?"

"It was weird. The women in my family all died really young, and most generations only had one male heir. I remember thinking it was strange as I fell asleep."

"It is strange, Aubrey."

"Yeah, it is, isn't it?"

It felt nice that Hank seemed to understand.

"And then what happened?" the sheriff prompted.

"The cat hissed and woke me up. Then I heard a really loud sound. It was a woman crying."

"A woman crying? Is there someone else here?"

"No."

"I see." Hank's brow furrowed.

"I walked toward the door leading up to the attic. The sound was coming from there. But I didn't have a flashlight, so I came downstairs to get one. That's when I smelled the smoke. I called you as I ran toward the sitting room, but then the door slammed shut, and I couldn't get out. When I woke up, you were here."

"You say the door to the sitting room was locked?"

"Yes. I couldn't get out. How did you get in?"

"It was standing wide open when I got here."

Aubrey racked her brain for a reasonable explanation. She felt an intense need to justify what had happened to her. But she had nothing.

"I need to look in the attic to make sure there's no one up there," Hank interjected.

"Okay. I'll go with you."

"Aubrey, you don't have to do that."

"I need to see it."

Hank nodded and grabbed his flashlight, and the pair ascended the winding staircase. They reached the second-floor landing and headed toward the door leading up to the attic. Aubrey felt strangely calm. Somehow it didn't seem as frightening as when she'd attempted to go up there alone.

Aubrey flipped on the light in the stairwell, but it didn't offer much assistance. Hank flicked his flashlight in front of them to add some illumination as they slowly crept up the creaking attic stairs. She fully expected to find someone there. The intensity of the sound of the woman crying had been jarring. Together, they searched the entire attic, even looking under the sheet-covered furniture in the center of the room. There was nothing.

"Something is wrong with me, Hank. I must have imagined it all," Aubrey said with a quivering voice.

"We'll figure it out. Let's go back downstairs now," he answered gently.

They left the attic and returned to the parlor on the first floor, where Aubrey sank dejectedly onto the sofa. There was nothing to figure out. There was no logical explanation.

Hank sat next to her on the sofa. "Aubrey, I know you don't understand what happened. I don't either. But I meant what I said. I don't think you're crazy."

"Well, that makes one of us. You know, I've never been the most stable person, but for the most part, I could tell the difference between illusion and reality. Ever since I've been in this house, I can't even do that." Aubrey's eyes filled with tears.

"I've heard stories about Desolate Ridge my whole life. My grandparents used to talk about the strange things that happened here. There are all kinds of legends, literally hundreds of them. I don't normally believe in ghost stories, but I've heard enough about this place to believe they're true," Hank explained.

"Are you telling me you believe Desolate Ridge is haunted?"

"I'm telling you I wouldn't rule it out."

Aubrey had wrestled with the haunted house theory, but she couldn't bring herself to give it any credence. If the townspeople believed it, perhaps there was a sliver of truth to the tales. After all, she'd experienced things she couldn't explain. The house was strange, and her family was even more bizarre. After reading the family Bible, she now had more questions than answers about the Rosses.

"You and your sister are the only people I've ever met who don't make me feel like a freak. You're both really kind. It must be in your DNA," Aubrey said. "Unfortunately, insanity runs in mine."

"I'm happy to do whatever I can. I mean that. I'd love to help you find the answers you need," Hank offered.

"I can't believe I'm about to say this, but I might take you up on that. I honestly have no idea where to start."

"My sister said you were joining us for dinner tomorrow."

"She said it wouldn't be a bother. I hope she was right."

"She was absolutely right. Maybe I could pick you up and drive you there?" Hank suggested. "That way you wouldn't have to try to find her house on your own."

The biggest part of Aubrey wanted to decline. It was the way she was wired; she didn't like asking for help, and she never let her guard down. But with Hank and Rebecca, something was different. For the first time in her life, she wasn't terrified of someone getting to know her, although she knew they would be shocked once they looked beneath the surface. Aubrey had some difficult baggage, after all, but the Metzgers' kindness made her want to try.

"All right, you can pick me up."

"You should think of some questions to ask my grandparents."

"I'll do that. I think I have about a million."

"I don't know the whole story, but there's some sort of connection between the Metzgers and the Rosses. Gramps will be able to tell you more," Hank explained.

"Really? That's interesting. I wonder what the connection is."

"It has something to do with the first woman who lived in this house."

"I look forward to hearing it. Honestly, I look forward to anything they're willing to tell me. No one around here will say anything. If only the walls could talk."

Aubrey rolled her eyes, and Hank laughed.

"Oh, Gramps is a talker. You'll have to beg him to stop. He's a sucker for a pretty face. That seems to run in the family too."

Hank's eyes lingered on hers. Aubrey would have been lying if she said the sheriff wasn't handsome, but her attraction went beyond the surface. There was a raw goodness about Hank. He radiated kindness. As much as she hated to admit it, he made her feel safe. No one had ever given her that feeling. It was confusing, but she liked it.

"Thanks again for coming to help me. I'm not good at asking for assistance, but I clearly needed it tonight."

"I don't like leaving you here alone. You're braver than I would be to stay here after being spooked like that."

"I've been alone my whole life, Hank. I've never known anything else."

"Well, maybe the tides are shifting. No one should be alone."

Aubrey tried to tear her gaze from his, but she couldn't. Thankfully, Hank looked away first, breaking the spell. He rose from the couch and headed toward the entryway. Aubrey followed.

"Promise you'll call me if you need help, Aubrey. I don't care what time it is."

"I promise. And thank you again."

They reached the front door, and Hank stepped outside. He wanted to stay with her. Something wasn't right inside that house. He could feel it. But it wasn't his place to insist. Hank had to believe Aubrey would reach out for help if she needed it.

He barely knew her, but he could see she didn't trust easily. If he pushed too hard, too quickly, she would fly away like a scared bird. That was the last thing he wanted, so he reluctantly returned to his patrol car.

Aubrey closed the door and went back inside. She was alone again, and it was the middle of the night. She hadn't slept for days, and although slumber wouldn't come easily, she needed to try.

Leaving the lights on, she returned upstairs to her bed and snuggled next to Spectre, glad to feel the warmth of the cat's body and hear the rhythmic sound of her purring.

Aubrey tossed and turned for a while, but she eventually drifted off to sleep.

The dream swirled into her subconscious, creeping in like a monster lurking in the shadows. A woman in a flowing white gown was running. It was the woman she'd dreamed of before, the same one she'd seen in the attic window. She recognized her immediately because the face was so much like her own.

The woman cried as she ran through the dark woods. Aubrey didn't know if she was running toward something or away from it. A man watched her go with a look of sadness that nearly ripped Aubrey's heart out. The man looked just like Hank, but his clothing was from another era.

As the woman ran, she cried, "Nothing hidden ever stays. It all ends with you."

When Aubrey woke the next morning, her pillow was soaked with tears. A pearl necklace and a freshly cut rose were lying on top of the family Bible. Neither had been there when she'd fallen asleep.

CHAPTER SEVENTEEN

Aubrey tentatively touched the rose. It was still wet with dew. The floral smell lingered in the room, cloying in its sweetness. She wondered if the flower was a figment of her imagination. She pressed her thumb against the thorn on the stem, and the sharp edge punctured her skin. Several drops of scarlet blood dripped onto her pillowcase. She shoved her thumb into her mouth, and the bitter taste of salt made her stomach flip.

The rose was real. But what did that mean? Who had put it there?

She sat up in bed and grabbed the pearl necklace, running her hands across the beads. The jewelry appeared to be quite old, and the size and luster of the pearls told her it was valuable. Neither item had been there when she'd gone to sleep, leaving Aubrey with only one conclusion—someone else had been in the house.

Aubrey hopped out of bed and dressed quickly. She was going to put an end to the madness, once and for all. She was tired of being afraid and confused. She needed answers, and the best place to find them was in the attic. After all, that was where she'd found the Bible. She had a feeling there were more secrets waiting for her if she could only be brave enough to search for them.

Spectre followed Aubrey as she climbed the attic stairs. She needed to get up there quickly, before she changed her mind; if she gave her plan too much thought, she'd talk herself out of it. Rather than listen to her fear, she pushed it aside, sprinting to the top of the stairs and flipping on the light switch. The morning sun filtered through the dirty attic windows. Aubrey glanced around the crowded room, trying to decide where to begin her search.

Her heart pounded. She feared what she might find, and yet she had to look. Taking a deep breath, she walked quickly across the room and flung open the doors of one of the large wardrobes. She gasped when she saw the closet was stuffed with fancy lace and silk ball gowns.

She fingered the delicate fabric, marveling at the fact that the dresses were at least a hundred years old. Other than being dusty, they were in perfect condition. She opened the wardrobe next to the first one and discovered more of the same. The styles of the gowns were different, and she estimated them to be even older than the others.

Breathing a little more easily, she turned her attention to the next tall wardrobe, expecting to find more clothing. Instead, she found a stack of large framed paintings standing on end. She counted them, noting seven in all. Curious, she grabbed the first painting and pulled it out of the wardrobe.

The piece of art was tall, reaching nearly to her waist when she placed it on the floor.

She crouched down and took a closer look. The painting had clearly been done by a skilled artist. It was amazingly realistic, almost like a photograph.

Aubrey didn't recognize the couple in the portrait. The woman was young and unsmiling. She had an austere countenance, and her jet-black hair was slicked back in a tight bun. She might have been beautiful if she hadn't looked so stern.

The man was about the same age. His scowling face stared at Aubrey from inside the frame. He had thick chestnut waves and sapphire eyes. He was quite handsome, but the grim look on his face was disconcerting. She had never seen such a frightening pair, and the sight of them gave her chills.

She leaned the portrait against the wall and grabbed the next one from the wardrobe. She gasped as she took a closer look. A stunning, dark-haired man sat in an ornately carved, finely upholstered armchair. His dark eyes glared menacingly at her. The evil look on the man's handsome face sent shivers down her spine. It was a face she'd never forget. He was the man from the nightmare she had on the plane.

Aubrey's hands flew to her throat. She could feel the man's spindly fingers wrapped around her neck, squeezing until there was no breath left. She could almost feel the heat from his hands as he tried to suffocate her.

The woman in the portrait wore a royal blue satin and

lace gown. Her flowing chestnut curls framed a sad, yet lovely face that was identical to Aubrey's. The woman's tiny left hand rested on the man's broad shoulder, the sapphire ring glittering on her finger.

It was the face that haunted her dreams, the same woman she'd seen twice in the attic window. She didn't know who the woman was, but Aubrey had felt her die. And the man in the portrait was the one who killed her.

Aubrey glanced through the remaining paintings. They all featured beautiful young women standing next to austere-looking men. Most of the portraits had a plain background, but one had been painted in front of the rose garden in the backyard. Despite the beauty of the blooming roses growing wildly behind them, the young couple's faces told a story of deep-seated sadness.

Another portrait grabbed her attention, featuring a lovely woman with golden curls. The artist had somehow caught her mid-laugh. Aubrey could almost hear the sound. The woman was lovely, but what Aubrey noticed first was the pearl necklace adorning her throat. It was the same piece of jewelry that was lying next to her bed that morning.

She needed to know more about the people in the portraits. She had to learn their stories in order to understand how the couples were connected to her. Why were the paintings hidden in a wardrobe in the attic? Why weren't they on display in the house?

Aubrey didn't know where to start, but it was time for her to call Mr. Lemon, the attorney. She should have done it sooner, but she had been preoccupied with trying to hold on to her sanity.

That hadn't turned out well.

One by one, Aubrey carried all the paintings downstairs to the sitting room. She searched through the drawer in the kitchen where she had stored Mr. Lemon's business card. With trembling fingers, she dialed his number. He answered on the first ring, almost as if he'd been awaiting her call. When she asked him to come over, he didn't hesitate, saying he would be there within the hour.

Not even thirty minutes later, his car pulled into the driveway. He knocked on the front door, and Aubrey answered it right away.

"You must be Ms. Ross," he said with a nod.

"You can call me Aubrey," she replied. "Please, come into the sitting room."

Obediently, Mr. Lemon followed. "I'm sure you have questions about the legal matters of the estate," he began.

"Right now I have more pressing matters, Mr. Lemon."

"More pressing than your financial issues?"

"Definitely."

Mr. Lemon seemed taken aback by her declaration. He had managed the affairs of Desolate Ridge for many years, and his employers had probably never been interested in anything besides money. Aubrey figured the man found it hard to believe that she would be all that different from her relatives, but his assumptions didn't matter to her in that moment.

"Well, Ms. Ross, now I'm intrigued. What matters are more pressing than your finances?"

"I need answers, and I don't know who else to ask."

"Answers about what?"

"My family."

"I'm not sure I can help."

Aubrey gestured toward the pictures she had leaned against the wall of the sitting room. Mr. Lemon's eyes widened when he saw them.

"I need to know about these paintings," she began.

"What would you like to know?"

"Who are they? I assume they're members of the Ross family."

Mr. Lemon took a deep breath, ruminating, appearing to contemplate his answer. His eyes darted back and forth between Aubrey and the paintings.

"They are your relatives, Ms. Ross."

"Do you know their names? Can you tell me anything at all about the paintings?"

Mr. Lemon sighed deeply and sat on the edge of the sofa. He removed his hat and placed it gingerly onto his lap, then pulled a handkerchief from out of his breast pocket and wiped the sweat that had pooled on his upper lip.

Aubrey took a seat in the armchair across from him, watching closely. She marveled at his mannerisms, recognizing he was clearly nervous. She didn't know what secrets the attorney was privy to, but he obviously knew something.

Aubrey waited for him to speak. After several minutes of awkward silence, he finally did.

"The paintings are wedding portraits."

"Wedding portraits?"

"Yes. The master of Desolate Ridge has always commissioned a wedding portrait as a present for the new mistress. They used to hang in the parlor until...."

He stopped for a moment and appeared to be weighing his words. There was clearly something he was avoiding, deftly skirting around issues of which he didn't want to speak.

"The portraits hung in the parlor until when, Mr. Lemon?" Aubrey coaxed gently.

"Your grandmother, Elizabeth, demanded they be removed."

"Why did she want them removed?"

"It was back when she started having her... episodes."

"Explain to me what you mean when you say episodes."

Mr. Lemon sighed. "Elizabeth said the paintings were talking to her, and she couldn't make them stop. She forced the Bonaventures to take them down and store them in the attic."

Aubrey let his words sink in before she spoke. Carlton had told Aubrey that the doctors believed her grandmother was schizophrenic, but Elizabeth insisted she wasn't. There was some kind of mental issue if her grandmother believed paintings were talking to her. Then again, Aubrey herself had seen a woman in the attic who had been dead for two hundred years.

"Mr. Lemon, can you tell me about the couples in the portraits?"

"I don't know all their names, but that particular painting

is of your grandparents."

Mr. Lemon stood and pointed to the first portrait Aubrey found. Apparently the angry woman with the black hair and severe bun was her grandmother, Elizabeth. The stern-looking man was her grandfather, Stuart. If they were as frightening as they appeared, it was no wonder Aubrey's mother had run away from home.

"And this one? Do you know their names?" Aubrey gestured toward the woman who could have been her twin and the man she'd seen in her nightmare.

"That was Marshall Ross and his wife, Marie. He had this house built for her. She was the first mistress of Desolate Ridge," Mr. Lemon explained.

"What happened to her? Can you tell me how she died?"

Aubrey knew it was a strange question, but she couldn't help it. She had seen firsthand how Marie Ross had died. She just needed someone to confirm it.

"I have no idea how she died, Ms. Ross. I'm not sure anyone does."

"Why is that?"

"Supposedly, Marie Ross disappeared. I don't know the details. The woman was a bit of a mystery."

"Well, I need to know about these people, Mr. Lemon," Aubrey insisted.

"I apologize, Ms. Ross, but I don't have the answers you're looking for."

"Oh, but I think you do. I am certain you know way more than you're telling me."

Mr. Lemon clamped his mouth shut tightly. It was clear that even if he did have information, he wasn't going to share it.

"Please, this is my life we're talking about. I need to know."

Mr. Lemon appeared to deliberate for a moment. Aubrey could see the man was at war with himself. She didn't understand why everyone was so secretive about the Ross family's history. Whatever had happened behind the walls of Desolate Ridge was buried so deeply that no one wanted to unearth it.

"I suppose you could talk to Clara Millburn. She's the town's historian. The library can tell you how to contact her. She might be able to help you," he replied tersely.

"I'll do that. Thank you."

"I have to go now. I just remembered that I have an appointment."

Aubrey was surprised at Mr. Lemon's strange reaction, as well as his abrupt, urgent need to leave. He placed his hat on his head, stood quickly from his seat, and practically ran toward the front door.

"I'll be in touch. We still need to discuss your financial situation, Ms. Ross."

"Just let me know when."

The man nodded as he nearly sprinted toward his car. He started it up and pulled out of the driveway quickly, flinging gravel as he went. Aubrey watched him leave, even more confused about why no one wanted to reveal the secrets of

Desolate Ridge.

Shaking her head, she walked into the kitchen to fix a sandwich. Propped against the kitchen counter was a shovel covered in fresh mud.

CHAPTER EIGHTEEN

Desolate Ridge
1920

"*Daddy, what are you doing? Where's Mama?" four-year-old James Ross cried on the portico.*

"Go back inside. I'll be there soon," Clarence yelled.

"But where's Mama? I want Mama!"

"Go!" Clarence screamed.

He watched his young son run back into the house, then looked down at the two bodies lying on the ground next to him. He wasn't sure what he would tell everyone, but he would come up with something. He always did. James would get over not having a mother, just as Clarence had. He'd suffered the loss at a young age as well.

Clarence's father, Peter, had been overbearing and angry, and Clarence had always believed it was because of the death of his mother, Catherine. She had died in a fire in the sitting room of Desolate Ridge when Clarence was just a year old. He would have died too, had his mother not broken the window and thrown him outside.

Catherine had been burned alive, and Clarence never knew the woman who had first given him life, then saved it. If he had, maybe he would have been different. Or perhaps he'd been damaged goods from the beginning. Sometimes he thought it would have been better if his mother had let him burn.

Clarence Ross dug the hole deeper. He picked up the whiskey bottle and chugged greedily, willing the liquid to chase away the voices in his foggy brain. He wiped the sweat that dripped from his forehead. Burying people was hard work. His arm muscles screamed for him to stop, but he couldn't. There was nothing to do but finish the job. The ground was soft from the recent spring rains, so that helped.

Clarence couldn't remember exactly what happened. How had he gotten to the place where he was digging holes to bury bodies? The last thing he could recall was the fury he'd felt when he came home and found the sheriff on the porch talking to his wife, Elsie.

That man had no business being around when Clarence wasn't home. It didn't matter that he was the sheriff. Elsie was Clarence's wife, and she belonged to him. The woman shouldn't have been talking to other men. Besides, the sheriff was too self-important. He'd needed to be taken down a notch. But Clarence couldn't remember much after that.

Clarence glanced at the ground where the two bodies lay side by side. He hadn't meant to take it that far, but when the rage came over him, he couldn't stop. Sometimes the whiskey helped, but sometimes it made things worse. This time, he'd blacked out completely, awakening to discover he'd lost control. So he had to dig two holes. He'd never imagined the possibility of having to dig two at the same time.

The rage came and went. Sometimes Clarence pretended to be a normal man. Sometimes he was able to convince people he was just like them. That's what he'd done with Elsie; she wouldn't have married him otherwise. But once he'd laid eyes on the woman, his only mission in life was to make her his. And he'd done it too. She'd wanted to be a rich man's wife, after all. He'd won out over the sheriff, who had also wanted Elsie. Clarence had won.

He leaned his weary body on the handle of the muddy shovel. He wished he could remember what had happened, but all he could recall was the rage that had followed him his whole life. It was a vicious cycle, the anger and the blackouts.

Taking another chug of whiskey, he looked at the bodies on the ground and tried to conjure up what had happened, but it was all a blank. Now he would have to make up a story to tell his son, James, to explain where his mother had gone.

Clarence Ross picked up the shovel and continued to dig the holes.

CHAPTER NINETEEN

Aubrey looked at the shovel leaning against her kitchen counter. She tentatively reached out and touched it. It was real. The wooden handle was worn and splintered, and the head was caked with fresh mud. She smelled the years of dirt and work on the tool.

She couldn't explain how it might have made its way into the house. She'd never seen it before. The Bonaventures hadn't arrived yet, so they couldn't have brought it in. The only person who had been in the house besides Aubrey was Mr. Lemon, and she'd been with him the entire time.

Aubrey paced back and forth across the kitchen floor, trying to come up with a possible answer. As hard as she tried, there wasn't one. Nor was there a reasonable explanation for the apparition in the attic, the frequent sounds of crying, a fire so real that she'd passed out from the smoke, or any of the other experiences she'd had since her arrival. The only conclusion was the one thing she feared the most—Aubrey was losing her mind.

It wasn't the first time she'd flirted with a mental breakdown. In fact, she'd had many episodes throughout her tumultuous life. She tried to think back to the techniques she'd learned from her various therapists. The one that always seemed to work for her was sensory grounding. Aubrey needed to focus on what was real, what she could experience through her senses. Those things were concrete, and if she homed in on the tangible, she would be able to center herself.

She tried to think of objects she could see, but the first thing that caught her eye was the muddy shovel. It was real. She could see it. But if that were the case, the only conclusion was that it had been put there by some kind of supernatural force. She refused to believe that was possible.

Aubrey moved on. She recalled things she could feel. She had felt the prick of the thorn from the rose that was beside her bed when she'd awakened that morning—the rose that hadn't been there when she'd fallen asleep. That was also real. She had the cut on her thumb to prove it. She'd tasted the blood.

She'd heard the keening wails from someone in the attic. She'd heard a woman's voice speaking to her when she'd arrived. Those things had been as real as the sound of Spectre's purr. But what did that mean? The sounds had all happened when there was no one in the house besides her. She also took into account the smell of smoke that was pungent enough to knock her out and powerful enough to cause her to call for help.

One by one, she moved through her senses, trying to

find one on which she could focus. She couldn't do it. She had seen, felt, heard, smelled, and tasted things that had no logical explanations. Grounding techniques had taught Aubrey that she could rely on her senses to tell her what was real. But her senses were telling her things she didn't want to believe.

Angry, Aubrey grabbed the shovel and stalked outside to the shed, opening the door and throwing the tool inside. It was time to face the fact that she'd had some sort of breakdown. That was easier than believing Desolate Ridge was haunted, as Hank seemed to think.

The thought of Hank caused Aubrey's mind to jump back to the night before. She'd been desperate and terrified, and she'd let down her guard with him. That wouldn't do. Aubrey could tell from the way Hank looked at her that he was interested in more than friendship, and she couldn't go down that road. It was a dead-end street.

Aubrey didn't do relationships. Yet in a moment of weakness, she'd agreed to some sort of date with Hank. That was a problem she needed to rectify immediately.

As she thought of his kind face, she felt a moment of guilt. Before it could settle in, she pushed it away. Hank was a nice guy, but maybe he was working some sort of angle. Maybe he wanted something from her. Or maybe he was the crazy one. After all, he'd told her he believed Desolate Ridge was haunted. Aubrey knew that couldn't be true. She didn't believe in ghosts.

It would be nice to have Rebecca for a friend, but she couldn't allow herself to get close to Hank. She wouldn't let it happen. She had to put an end to the possibility. Aubrey grabbed her phone from her pocket and dialed his number. He answered on the third ring.

"Hey, Aubrey," he said casually.

"Hello. You don't need to pick me up tonight. I've changed my mind. I'll drive myself," she blurted.

"I really don't mind. I was looking forward to it, in fact."

His voice reminded her of the safety she'd felt with him. She hesitated for a moment. Maybe she was being hasty. It wouldn't be that big of a deal to let him drive her to dinner. Maybe they could just be friends. As soon as the thoughts entered her mind, though, she chased them away. She had enough baggage in her life without adding to it.

"Thanks, but no thanks. I can drive myself."

"All right. If that's what you want, Aubrey."

She heard the disappointment through the phone line. She reminded herself it didn't matter. There could be nothing between them.

"This is what I want."

"I'll see you later, then. Drive safely."

"Goodbye."

She hung up quickly before she could change her mind. Her hands shook as she dropped the phone back into her pocket. She didn't want to hurt him, but she couldn't let him get attached. She could tell from a mile away that Hank was the sort of man who cared deeply about people. That just didn't work for her. It was better to stop things before they started.

If she hadn't wanted the information the Metzgers might

provide, she wouldn't even go to the dinner. But Rebecca said her family had been in Rossdale for hundreds of years. Hank had told her his family had some sort of connection to hers. No one besides the Metzgers wanted to tell her anything. Aubrey needed to talk to them. Family dinner seemed to be a necessary evil if she wanted to find out more about Desolate Ridge.

CHAPTER TWENTY

Aubrey sat in the driveway of Rebecca's house, trying to catch her breath. She hadn't expected to have a panic attack in the car, yet that's exactly what happened when she arrived. She should have known it was a mistake to go.

As she rocked back and forth in the driver seat, trying to calm herself with the repetitive rhythm, Aubrey wondered again why she'd believed she should go to Rebecca's house. She stared through the large windows into a room filled with people she'd never seen. They were laughing and talking, so comfortable with one another that it made her heart ache.

Aubrey wondered what that kind of connection might feel like. She'd never been close to anyone. She didn't belong in a room like that. She didn't belong anywhere. Her loneliness consumed her, nearly drowning her in its vastness. She wished things were different, but being by herself was reality.

She wanted the information the Metzgers might be able to provide, but that didn't matter. She couldn't bring herself to get out of her car and go inside. She didn't know how to talk to people. She had no idea how to function in what appeared to be a picture-perfect family environment. Aubrey wasn't cut out for such things, and it would be best if she just went home.

Turning the key in the ignition, she started the car once again. As she did, she was startled by a knock on the window. She turned her head to see Rebecca standing there, a wide smile on her friendly face. Aubrey slowly rolled down her window.

"Hey there. You're not leaving already, are you?"

The wide grin on Rebecca's face disappeared quickly when she saw the look of anguish on Aubrey's.

"Yeah, I am. I can't do this," Aubrey answered as her eyes filled with tears.

"You don't have to do anything. Just come inside," Rebecca gently coaxed.

"You don't understand. It's just… I don't know how… to do… family things."

"Look, Aubrey, I could lie and say I understand, but the truth is I don't. But I like you. Let me be your friend."

"It sounds so simple when you say it," Aubrey grumbled.

"But it's not simple for you at all, is it?"

"Rebecca, socializing is such a complex idea that I can't even wrap my brain around what it means. I've been alone my whole life, and no one has ever cared. The thought of walking into your house and talking to your family seems like an insurmountable obstacle to me. I'm sure that sounds silly to you."

"It doesn't sound silly. And I'm sorry that being alone has been your reality. I'd like to help change that."

Rebecca took one giant step away from the car, giving Aubrey the space to make what was clearly a difficult decision.

"But I don't know how to talk to people. I always say stupid things," Aubrey explained.

"You don't have to say anything at all. Or you can talk for an hour without coming up for air if you want to. There are no judgments or expectations here. Will you come inside?"

Rebecca extended her hand. Aubrey hesitated. It would be so much easier to turn the car around and drive home.

Aubrey looked through the large window of Rebecca's house once again. Everyone was crowded around the television in the living room, looking comfortable and at ease with one another. Something tugged at Aubrey's heart, a sense of longing she couldn't explain.

What if?

"All right."

"You mean you'll come in?"

"I'll come in. But I'm warning you that I'm the most socially awkward person in the world, Rebecca, and you're going to immediately regret having me here."

"That's not even a possibility."

Aubrey rolled up the window, turned off the ignition, and slowly climbed out of the vehicle. Rebecca reached out and grabbed her hand, grasping it tightly inside her own.

"You shouldn't have to do hard things alone, Aubrey. My family is loud and annoying, but they're excited to meet you."

Aubrey apprehensively followed Rebecca into the family room, steeling herself for the same cold reaction she'd received from the other people in Rossdale. She couldn't have been more wrong. One by one, Rebecca introduced Aubrey to each member of the Metzger family. Each one smiled kindly, welcoming her with open arms. She'd never before experienced such a level of complete and total acceptance.

Aubrey met George and Helen, who were Hank and Rebecca's parents, as well as Hank Sr. and Sharlene, their grandparents. She made the official acquaintance of Jake, Rebecca's husband and the cook from the restaurant. Aubrey congratulated him on making the best french toast she'd ever tasted.

"I hope you'll enjoy dinner just as much," Jake said with a laugh. "I've made my famous pot roast."

"It sounds delicious."

"It is," Jake replied with a grin and a shrug.

Aubrey noticed Hank sitting on the couch and her stomach flipped. She felt terrible about the epic brush-off she'd given him, but it couldn't be helped. Rather than treating her as she probably deserved, he stood and welcomed her with a smile.

"Hey, Aubrey. I see you found your way."

"I did."

She could have said more, but it was best to leave things alone. Hank brought up far too many conflicting emotions that she didn't understand.

"Now that we're all here, let's go eat. My pot roast is waiting," Jake announced.

She followed the Metzgers into the dining room and hesitated as they all took their seats. She wasn't sure where she was supposed to sit.

"Your spot is right here, between me and Hank," Rebecca instructed as she patted the seat next to her.

Aubrey nodded and took her seat, glancing around the table at the faces before her. She'd expected to feel anxious, but instead she felt calm. She didn't know what sort of magic ran through the Metzger DNA, but whatever it was, she liked it.

They plated up Jake's delicious food, and the conversation never lagged. Aubrey didn't join in; she simply observed and listened while the family talked. No one pestered her with awkward small talk, and no one put her on the spot with invasive questions. They seemed to understand and respect her unspoken boundaries.

When Jake passed out the dessert, strawberry cheesecake, Aubrey finally worked up the nerve to speak. After all, that was why she'd come. She directed her question to George, Helen, Sharlene, and Hank Sr.

"So, Hank and Rebecca have told me you might have some information about Desolate Ridge. I've questioned everyone I can think of, and no one will talk."

"What do you know already?" Sharlene asked gently.

"Not much. I arrived in Rossdale right after finding out I'd inherited the house. I've tried asking the housekeepers, the driver, and the attorney, but no one will tell me anything.

The moment I mention my family, everyone either clams up or runs away," Aubrey answered.

"I'm sorry you've had such a rough go of it, dear. That sounds quite frustrating," Helen answered sympathetically.

"To say the least," Aubrey agreed. "That's why I'm here. When Rebecca said you might know something about my family, I had to find out."

"I went to school with your mother. I have to say you look just like her. The resemblance is uncanny, actually," Helen said with a smile.

"You knew her?"

"I knew Anna in passing. We didn't really run in the same circles. Then she quit school and was tutored at home after you were born," Helen explained.

"Did you know my father too?"

Aubrey had no idea if anyone knew who her father was, but she was willing to try.

"There were rumors, but I really don't know," Helen answered.

"What were the rumors?"

"Your grandparents were unreasonably strict. Anna wasn't allowed to associate with anyone from school. She certainly wasn't allowed to date. Her parents didn't think anyone was good enough for her. I always heard they didn't approve of your father, so they forbade her from seeing him, even after you were born. Evidently he wasn't up to your grandparents' standards, not that anyone was. Eventually Anna ran away. I never heard what happened to her. I always wondered if she left because of her parents."

"My mother abandoned me at a hospital in Seattle when I was three. She killed herself not long after that. That's the extent of what I know about her," Aubrey answered quietly.

Hank gasped, and Rebecca leaned over and put her arm around Aubrey's shoulder.

"Oh, honey, I had no idea," Helen replied kindly.

"It's water under the bridge now. Please don't feel sorry for me," Aubrey said stiffly.

There was nothing worse than hearing pity in another person's voice. That was one thing she couldn't endure.

"It's not pity, Aubrey. It's sadness for what you've experienced. There's a difference," Helen explained. "No child should ever be abandoned."

Aubrey didn't know what to say. She'd never felt such genuine emotion. Yet there she was, surrounded by it. It was a lot to process.

Uncomfortable with the attention, Aubrey cleared her throat. "Is there anything else you can tell me?"

"I've heard stories about Desolate Ridge and the Ross family for as long as I can remember. I'm sure you've figured out by now that most of the tales aren't happy ones. Dad can probably tell you the most." George nodded toward his father, Hank Sr.

"Anything at all would be more than I already know, sir," Aubrey said to the older man.

"I'll tell you what I know, on one condition," Hank Sr. began.

"What's the condition?" Aubrey asked timidly.

"That you never call me 'sir' again. It makes me feel like

an old man," he replied with a hearty laugh.

Aubrey grinned, surprised by his request. "What should I call you, then?"

"Well, most folks call me Gramps, so you should too." He grinned.

"If you insist," Aubrey responded.

"I do."

"Wasn't there some sort of connection between the Rosses and the Metzgers, Gramps?" Hank chimed in.

"Oh, yes, there certainly was. The Metzgers have crossed paths with the Rosses for generations. Why, the first woman who lived in Desolate Ridge was actually in love with a Metzger."

"Do you mean Marie?" Aubrey couldn't believe she might finally get some information about the woman who incessantly haunted her house, her thoughts, and her dreams.

"My grandpa used to tell me a story that his grandpa told him. Apparently my fourth-great-grandfather, Henry, was in love with a local girl named Marie Stockton. They intended to marry, but her parents promised her to Marshall Ross instead. Marie didn't want to marry Marshall. In fact, she was terrified of the man. Marshall's sister, Eleanor, disappeared mysteriously after their parents died. When she left, Marshall got everything. Marie wasn't interested in his money, but her parents were. They forced her to go through with the wedding. Both Henry and Marie were heartbroken. Henry later went on to marry someone else, thank goodness, or none of us would be here," Hank Sr. chuckled.

"So the first mistress of Desolate Ridge was in love with

a Metzger. She didn't want to marry Marshall Ross at all. That explains why she always looks so sad," Aubrey said quietly.

"She always looks sad? You mean you've seen her?" Hank asked with a wrinkled brow.

"Oh… her… portrait. I've… seen her picture."

Aubrey tried to cover her mistake. She couldn't have the Metzgers knowing she'd seen a woman who had been dead for two centuries.

"I have an old painting of Henry. It's hanging in the sitting room. I'll show you before you leave," Rebecca added.

"I would love to see it," Aubrey replied. Then she turned to Hank Sr. "Is there anything else you can tell me?"

"There have always been stories that Desolate Ridge is haunted. People in town say it has something to do with Marshall, who built the house. His sister vanished under questionable circumstances, his parents died suspiciously, and Marie was never found either. She just disappeared one day. I always thought it was odd that a woman would leave when she had a small child," he shared.

"Yes, that does seem strange. But then again, none of the deaths of the women in my family quite add up," Aubrey began.

"What do you mean?" Rebecca asked.

"I found an old family Bible. It listed all of the births, deaths, and marriages. Other than my grandmother, Elizabeth, every woman in my family has died by the age of twenty-five. I'm not a doctor, but that doesn't sound like natural causes to me. It also doesn't bode well for my future, considering I'm twenty-five." Aubrey laughed nervously.

"I'm sure you have nothing to worry about," Rebecca said kindly as she patted Aubrey's hand.

"I don't know. It's pretty worrisome," she replied. "I swear it's like that house will do anything to hold on to its secrets."

"Don't fret, dear. Nothing hidden ever stays," Sharlene said with a smile.

"What did you say?"

Aubrey's heart nearly stopped as Sharlene repeated the same phrase she'd heard Marie say in her dream.

"I said that nothing hidden ever stays," Sharlene repeated.

"What do you mean by that?"

"I just mean everything is eventually brought to light. Secrets don't stay hidden forever."

"Yes… of course. You're right."

Aubrey tried to hide the fact that she was rattled. It was purely coincidental that Sharlene had spoken the exact words from the dream. Surely it meant nothing.

"Wasn't there something about your great-grandpa and Desolate Ridge, Dad?" George asked.

"Yes, there was, as a matter of fact. My great-grandpa, Howard, was the sheriff of Rossdale. He went missing around 1920. He was sweet on Elsie Willard, who married Clarence Ross. Everyone was surprised when Elsie married Clarence instead of Howard. Anyhow, Howard was out patrolling one day, and no one ever saw him again. His car was found near Desolate Ridge, although none of the Ross family or their servants could recall him being at the house," Hank Sr. answered.

"It seems like the Metzger men have a knack for getting involved with the women in your family line, Aubrey," George teased.

"It never seems to end well for them, does it?" Aubrey stole a glance at Hank. The strange history between their families was just one more reason why Aubrey should keep her distance from him.

"So the mystery of Sheriff Howard's disappearance was never solved?" she asked.

"No, it wasn't. We don't know what happened to Grandpa Howard. That's actually one of the reasons why I became a sheriff. No one's family should experience that kind of uncertainty about a loved one," Hank explained.

"Our Hank keeps the citizens of Rossdale safe, don't you, little brother?" Rebecca teased with a grin.

"I do my best, if they'll let me," he replied with a sideways look at Aubrey.

Her face flushed. She knew he was talking about her. Thankfully no one else at the table seemed to pick up on it.

They finished dessert, and Aubrey carried her plate to the kitchen. She offered to help with the dishes, but Jake refused.

"You're our guest. You don't need to do dishes," he insisted.

"I told you I would show you the painting of Henry. Come with me." Rebecca grabbed Aubrey's hand and led her down the hall into the sitting room. "There it is."

Hanging above the large fireplace was a very old painting. It looked to have been commissioned around the same time as the one of Marie and Marshall that she'd found at Desolate Ridge. The painting featured a handsome young man in hunting gear. Aubrey couldn't believe her eyes.

"That's Henry Metzger? The man who was in love with Marie?"

"It is," Rebecca replied.

"He looks just like Hank." Aubrey exhaled sharply.

"Yes, he does."

The man in the portrait was the spitting image of Hank, but that wasn't the only thing that surprised Aubrey. The hunting clothes were the same ones worn by the man in her dream—the man she now understood was Henry Metzger. Hank's relative was the person whose face was covered in sadness as he watched Marie run away into the woods.

CHAPTER TWENTY-ONE

"Is something wrong, Aubrey? You seem startled by the painting." Rebecca gently placed her hand on Aubrey's arm.

"I'm just surprised by how much he looks like your brother."

"Yeah, the resemblance is bizarre, right?"

Aubrey wished she could tell Rebecca about the man in her dream, but she couldn't. It didn't make sense, and Aubrey herself was still trying to wrap her brain around it. To add to the strangeness, Aubrey looked exactly like Marie, the woman Henry loved.

"I don't mean to scare you, but I think my brother likes you," Rebecca revealed with a grin.

"Why would you think that? Did he say something to you?"

Aubrey tried to still her pounding heart. The last thing she needed was her new friend playing matchmaker with her brother.

"No, Hank wouldn't tell me, even if he did. He's a bit

gun-shy with women ever since Hillary."

"Who's Hillary?"

Aubrey wasn't interested in Hank. Not in the least. But in spite of herself, she was curious about his past. She wanted to know more.

"Hillary was Hank's high school sweetheart. They were together for a long time. Everyone thought they would be married by now. They were engaged for two years," Rebecca answered.

"What happened?"

"She took off a year ago, told Hank she had to get out of Rossdale. She wasn't cut out for small-town life, I suppose. She thought she was better than us country bumpkins. She went to Los Angeles to try her hand at acting. It totally broke Hank's heart."

Aubrey winced. "Ouch. Poor Hank."

"Yeah, he was pretty torn up about it. He's just now starting to get back to normal. That's how I know he likes you. He hasn't glanced twice at another woman in years, but he sure was checking you out at dinner."

"I hope you're wrong, Rebecca."

"You don't think Hank's cute? I mean, he's my brother and all, but he's pretty easy on the eyes. He's also the kindest man I've ever known."

Aubrey noted the defensiveness in Rebecca's voice, and she realized her friend completely misunderstood. Hank wasn't lacking in anything. It was the other way around. Aubrey was the one who had nothing to offer. Any ideas about the two of them becoming a couple had to be squashed immediately.

"Hank is great. Really. I'm the problem," Aubrey explained.

"What do you mean? Are you already involved with someone?"

"Oh, goodness, no. Nothing like that."

"Then what is it?"

"Rebecca, I don't do relationships of any kind. Ever. I've had exactly two boyfriends in my life. I'm not sure you'd even call them that," Aubrey admitted.

"And what happened with them?"

"Not much. I ended both of them before they could evolve into relationships. My therapists have all said that fear of commitment is common in people who were abandoned as small children. I figured out pretty early on that the only person I could depend on was me. It's just easier that way."

"Do you mind talking about it?" Rebecca asked hesitantly.

"About my life?"

"I'm sorry, of course you mind talking about it. I'm sure it's incredibly painful. That was a stupid question."

"It wasn't stupid."

"Yes it was. It was dumb and invasive."

"Look, I don't usually talk about it, but… what do you want to know?" Aubrey offered.

"You said you were only three when your mother left you. Did you ever find out why she did it?"

"I always imagined that Anna was a horrible, selfish girl, but I don't think that anymore."

"Why is that?"

"Well, I think she was probably suffering from depression or something. She killed herself, and people who knew her said she was always unhappy. I'm learning that mental illness seems to run rampant in my family," Aubrey explained.

"Why do you think that?"

"I'm assuming my mother suffered from depression or some sort of anxiety, and I was told my grandfather died in a mental institution. My grandmother was diagnosed with schizophrenia, although apparently she disagreed with the label. I'm beginning to wonder how much deeper it goes," Aubrey answered.

"What about you?"

"You mean am I crazy too?" Aubrey smirked.

"Well, not exactly in those words. It just seems to me that someone with your background couldn't have escaped without some wounds."

"You're right. I guess I kind of teeter somewhere between illusion and reality. I live in my head a lot. The things I imagine are always better than real life. I've never asked for a diagnosis because I've always wanted to avoid labels, but I'll be the first to admit I have issues."

"Issues?"

"Yeah, I've struggled with anxiety, depression, a bit of paranoia. I don't know if any of it is hereditary, or if it was all brought on by my circumstances. You know, the old 'nature versus nurture' argument. I spent most of my childhood in therapists' offices. One of my foster parents even wanted to have an exorcism performed."

Aubrey chuckled and rolled her eyes. The look on Rebecca's face made it clear that her friend didn't find anything funny about the concept.

"An exorcism? Aubrey, you must be joking."

"Unfortunately, no. Some people are frightened when a kid insists bad things are going to happen before they do. It's even scarier when those things come to pass. I learned to just keep my mouth shut."

Rebecca's eyes widened. "You mean you have premonitions?"

"Something like that. I usually know when something bad is coming. I always have some sort of physical reaction."

"Physical reaction?"

"I get goose bumps, the hair on the back of my neck prickles, and my eye twitches."

"Really?"

"Yeah. I also see things sometimes... especially since coming to Desolate Ridge."

"What kind of things?"

"You wouldn't believe me if I told you."

Aubrey rolled her eyes. She was certain Rebecca wasn't far from reaching the conclusion that Aubrey was too crazy to be her friend.

"Try me. You might be surprised at what I'm willing to believe, Aubrey."

"Well, I've had strange encounters in different rooms of the house. They're intense, surreal moments. They're honestly terrifying. It's like I'm experiencing horrible things that have happened to other people. The feelings are so strong. It's almost as if during the episodes, I actually become another person. I experience these terrible moments inside their skin."

Aubrey laughed derisively. "Now's the time when you tell me I'm off my rocker."

"I think there are some things that can't be explained by logic, Aubrey."

"You sound like your brother now. Hank actually told me he thinks Desolate Ridge is haunted."

"Anyone who grew up in Rossdale believes Desolate Ridge is haunted," Rebecca explained.

As if they had conjured him out of thin air with their words, Hank appeared, sticking his head into the room.

"Hey, ladies, I'm going to go home now."

"Bye, little brother." Rebecca blew a kiss in his direction. "Thanks for coming."

"You know I never pass up a chance to eat Jake's pot roast. It was good to see you again, Aubrey."

"You too, Hank."

She glanced in his direction, and their eyes met. The strange, familiar sense of safety enveloped her. She couldn't explain it, and she tried to ignore it, but it was undeniably real.

She looked back to her friend. "I'm going to head home too, Rebecca. Thanks again for the meal and the information."

"You're welcome anytime, Aubrey. I mean that. Hey, Hank, will you do me a favor?" Rebecca asked as she turned toward her brother.

"Anything for you, sis." Hank grinned.

"Follow Aubrey home. It's raining, and I don't like her being on the road alone."

"He doesn't need to—"Aubrey began.

"Humor me. Please. I'm a worrier," Rebecca insisted.

"I honestly don't mind, Aubrey. I'm going your way anyhow," Hank interjected.

Unsure of what else to do, and not wanting to make unnecessary waves, Aubrey agreed to the arrangement.

"Is this what it's like to have friends? I suppose it might grow on me eventually," she relented.

"Yes, this is what it means to have friends. I think you'll like it."

"I'll have to take your word for it," Aubrey replied.

Rebecca wrapped her arms around Aubrey and hugged her tightly.

"Aubrey, I think you're wonderful to have survived being abandoned and growing up alone. You are my new hero."

"I'm no one's hero, Rebecca."

Aubrey awkwardly returned Rebecca's hug and then took a decisive step away from her friend.

"Then we'll agree to disagree, because I think you're pretty amazing."

Rebecca walked her to the front door. Aubrey said goodbye to the Metzgers, thanking them for the information about her family. After that, she thanked Jake for dinner, and then she and Hank walked toward her car.

Aubrey wanted to tell the sheriff to leave her alone. She wanted to insist she didn't need an escort. She wanted to scream at him to stop confusing her with emotions she didn't understand. But Aubrey didn't say a word, because deep down, that insecure girl inside of her craved the feeling of shelter he provided. It was dangerous ground, and she was dancing on a minefield.

"I hope the information my family gave you will help," Hank said as he opened her car door.

"It will. I'm more determined than ever. Something isn't right. My mother mentioned a family curse in her suicide note. At first, I laughed it off, but I'm beginning to think there might be something to it," Aubrey answered.

"I told you before that I'll help you. The offer still stands."

"I'm not used to having help. I do things on my own, Hank." Aubrey slid into the driver seat.

"Maybe it's time to try a different approach."

"Maybe."

Aubrey shrugged as tears glistened in her eyes. She was so confused. It would be comforting to have someone on her side. She'd never craved companionship before, but something about Hank made her want it so badly, it nearly broke her heart.

Hank didn't push Aubrey farther. He didn't take advantage of her vulnerability and confusion. Instead, he closed her car door, waited for her to pull out of the driveway, and then followed closely behind her in his patrol car.

When Aubrey's BMW reached the driveway of Desolate

Ridge, Hank watched her vehicle disappear into the forested twists and turns. He hesitated for a brief moment, wanting to follow her, to help her. But he didn't. In time, he hoped she would trust him.

CHAPTER TWENTY-TWO

"I've finished polishing the floors in the library, Aubrey," Mrs. Bonaventure said as she came into the kitchen.

"Thank you. I think the floor in the sitting room will need polishing as well. I want the house ready to be shown within the next few weeks. I have an appointment today with Mr. Lemon, so I should have concrete details after that."

Aubrey took a sip of her coffee and tried to ignore the look of disapproval on the housekeeper's face.

"You're really going to sell Desolate Ridge?" Mrs. Bonaventure frowned, not hiding her displeasure.

"I have no reason not to sell it, Mrs. Bonaventure."

"Well, perhaps you'll find one."

"Is it so wrong that I don't want it? I understand the house has been in the Ross family for two hundred years, but that doesn't mean anything to me. I didn't even know about it until a few weeks ago, and I can't imagine living here for the rest of my life."

"There are things you need to understand about this

house and your family, Aubrey." Mrs. Bonaventure fiddled with her apron and chewed her lip nervously.

"Like what? How am I supposed to understand anything when no one will tell me?" Aubrey placed her hands on her hips and glared at the older woman.

Mrs. Bonaventure simply shook her head. Aubrey knew the woman wanted to say more, but of course, she didn't. Just as the house held on to its secrets, so did Mrs. Bonaventure.

"Aubrey, will you come take a look at the hedge to see if you like the changes I've made?" Anson popped his head into the kitchen.

"Lead the way," Aubrey replied, happy to be free of Mrs. Bonaventure's lecture.

She followed Anson around the house and through the backyard. She had only spoken to him a few times, but she'd experienced the same strange, unexplainable feeling on each and every occasion. When she looked at him, she felt connected, as if they were tethered by an invisible rope. Being around Anson made her both sad and uncomfortable.

"I thought it would look better if I trimmed the top. Do you like it?" Anson motioned toward the tall hedge, which he'd expertly sculpted to perfection.

"It looks great. You're very good at what you do. Thank you, Anson," Aubrey said with a grin.

"Your smile lights up your face."

"What did you say?"

"I used to tell your mother the same thing." Anson's voice was so quiet, Aubrey almost couldn't hear it.

"Everyone says my mother was always sad. Did you know her well?"

"Anna wasn't always sad. There was another side to her. It didn't come out often, but I saw it."

"Were the two of you friends? I've heard she didn't have many."

"That's because your grandparents tried to control every second of her life. But they couldn't. Stuart and Elizabeth couldn't control Anna, and it angered them when she made decisions on her own. "

The fire in his voice surprised her. It was as if the words had been percolating inside of him for years, waiting for the right moment to bubble free.

"Do you mean the decision my mother made to run away?"

"I mean the reason she was forced to run away in the first place. They left her no choice, you know."

"No choice about what, Anson?"

He stared right into Aubrey's eyes. "About you. She left to protect you."

"Protect me from what?"

"They were going to take you away from Anna. They were going to force her to give you up. They locked the two of you inside her room. The servants were told to give you food and water, but nothing more."

"What?" Aubrey couldn't believe what she was hearing. It couldn't be true.

"I heard Anna banging on the door, screaming to come out. It was awful. I tried to get help. I told my mother she had

to do something. She said she would talk to my father—"
Anson's voice cracked with emotion.

"What about your father?"

"I can't...."

Aubrey didn't want to push him to the point that he
stopped talking, so she didn't force him to continue. She
gave him a moment to compose himself as she tried to
process the awful details Anson had thrown at her. In the
letter, Anna had called Desolate Ridge a madhouse. Aubrey
assumed it was an exaggeration. Maybe it wasn't.

"Why would my grandparents do that to their own
daughter and grandchild?"

"Because they were insane. Haven't you figured that out
by now?"

"Why should I believe you? If things were really as
bad as you say, someone would have stopped Stuart and
Elizabeth, right? They wouldn't allow them to get away
with imprisoning me and my mother."

Anson scoffed. "You have no idea who the Rosses were,
Aubrey. You can't imagine the kind of power they wielded.
People were terrified of them, especially their employees."

"How did my mother escape?"

"She tricked her parents into believing she would give
you away, so they let her out. When Stuart and Elizabeth
let their guard down, Anna ran. She was penniless. She ran
away with nothing except you. I didn't even know she was
leaving—"

"Anson, I need your help in here. There's a vase I can't
reach on my own," Mrs. Bonaventure called from the kitchen

door, interrupting the conversation at a critical moment.

"What were you going to say, Anson?"

"Nothing. Forget about it. I've said too much already."

He turned abruptly and headed back into the house. Aubrey watched him go, wishing he would have said more.

A feeling of sadness washed over her. If what Anson said was true, her mother cared for her more than she'd ever imagined. Anna had escaped in order to save her.

Guilt and confusion played tug-of-war inside Aubrey's heart. Nothing about Anna Ross was anything like she'd believed. Aubrey's entire life felt like one gigantic lie after another. Not knowing what else to do, she returned to the kitchen.

"Mr. Lemon just called to cancel your appointment this afternoon. He said he would call back to reschedule. Apparently something came up," Mrs. Bonaventure explained when Aubrey entered.

"Thank you. That's probably for the best," Aubrey replied listlessly.

"Are you feeling all right? You don't look well."

"It's this house. I need to sell it. I have to get out of here."

"You can't run away from your problems, Aubrey. Otherwise, you'll never stop running. You're looking for answers. You need to find them." Mrs. Bonaventure placed her warm hand over Aubrey's cold one.

"If you feel that way, why won't you help me? Your family has worked at Desolate Ridge for years. Surely you know things you aren't telling me. Why won't anyone help me?" Tears of desperation brimmed in Aubrey's eyes.

"Aubrey, you don't understand. There are things I... can't say. I can't. I've kept secrets to protect the people I care about." Mrs. Bonaventure's eyes grew wide with fear and desperation.

"Protect them from what? In case you haven't noticed, there's no one here but me. Whoever you were trying to protect, it doesn't matter anymore," Aubrey demanded.

"They said they would kill him. I couldn't let them know the truth."

Mrs. Bonaventure sank into a nearby chair and began to sob.

"Who are you talking about, Mrs. Bonaventure?"

"My boy. They said they would kill my boy!"

"Someone threatened Anson? I'm sure it was a misunderstanding. Surely whoever said it didn't mean it."

"It wasn't a threat, and I didn't misunderstand. They meant every word they ever said."

"Who?"

"Your grandparents!" Mrs. Bonaventure screamed the words, her body heaving as if they had been dragged out of her. As soon as she spoke, she clamped her hand over her mouth to prevent any other information from escaping.

"Stuart and Elizabeth threatened you? They threatened Anson?"

"I shouldn't have said anything. I swore I wouldn't."

"Enough secrets! I've had enough. You will tell me exactly what you know, and you'll do it now," Aubrey commanded, summoning every ounce of authority she possessed.

The woman wrung her hands, clearly frightened. Aubrey didn't back down. She glared at Mrs. Bonaventure until the older woman spoke again.

"I'm sorry, Aubrey. I should have been stronger. When she told me, I should have helped her instead of being a coward, but I was afraid for my son."

"Who should you have helped?"

"Your mother came to me before she ran away. She told me that... that Anson was your... your father, and instead of helping the poor child, I panicked. Your grandparents said if they found out who your father was, they would kill him. I knew they weren't just words. They would have done it. I should have helped Anna. If I had, maybe things would have been different... for her and for you," Mrs. Bonaventure explained.

"Anson is my father? He knew, and he let us leave?"

"He didn't know," she replied quickly.

"How is that possible?"

Anger bubbled up inside of Aubrey. She had always believed Anna was the selfish one, but apparently it was Anson.

"I swear to you that my son didn't know. He suspected, of course, but Anna put an end to that. The two of them were in love. He would have gone with her, or talked her into staying. And your grandparents would have killed him if they knew," she rambled.

"My mother didn't tell him? How could he not have known if they were in love like you say?"

"Anson was away at college when Anna found out she

was pregnant. She didn't tell him. She hid it from everyone for as long as she could. When he came home, she was nearly ready to give birth. Her parents told her they would kill the father of her child once they figured out who he was. Anna knew they would do it. Anson believed it was him, but Anna told him she'd been with someone else. Turns out, she only said that to protect him. She kept the secret for two years, up until she left with you. That day, she told me Anson was your father. She asked for my help. I failed her. And you," she finished between sobs.

"So Anson really doesn't know he's my... father?" The word sounded foreign on her tongue.

Aubrey should have been surprised by the news, yet she wasn't. She had felt an undeniable connection to Anson Bonaventure, and now she understood why. It was as if Mrs. Bonaventure simply confirmed something she already knew.

"Anson still believes Anna betrayed him with someone else. He loved her so much. I don't think he ever got over it. He'll hate me once he discovers I knew the truth. I'm sure you hate me. I hate myself. I won't even ask for your forgiveness, because I don't deserve it."

"You're right. You don't."

Aubrey's hands began to shake, and tears coursed down her face. She despised the emotions that were swimming to the surface, yet she couldn't push them down or compartmentalize them no matter how hard she tried.

"I can't do this right now. I don't even know what to say to you."

Aubrey paced back and forth across the kitchen floor.

"I'm sorry—"

"I don't want to hear your meager apologies, you horrible, selfish woman. But you will tell Anson the truth, and you will tell him today. If you don't, I will, and I will not be kind."

Without another word, Aubrey stalked out of the kitchen and ran up the winding staircase toward her bedroom. Slamming the door behind her, she flung herself onto the large four-poster bed and sobbed.

She wasn't a crier. She never had been. She was tough, and she was hard. That's how she survived. But in that moment, she was nothing more than the abandoned little girl who was left at a hospital alone without a soul in the world to care.

Every emotion she'd ever suppressed mixed together, combining into a melting pot of quicksand that swallowed her up inside. She was stuck in the quagmire, and she felt herself sinking. She cried for all of the times she hadn't. She cried for the countless years she'd spent being passed around from one family to the next, each one worse than the last, none of them ever wanting her.

She cried for the abuse she'd endured, for the isolation she'd worn until it wrapped around her like her own skin. She cried for the injustice of it all, because she wasn't an orphan. She never had been. She had a father and grandparents who had allowed horrible things to happen to her.

It wasn't fair.

When she'd finally spent all of her tears, she lay there, exhausted. Weary to the bone, her traumatized body finally gave in to sleep. She dreamed of her mother. She saw her running away from Desolate Ridge, young, afraid, clutching Aubrey's small body close to her own.

She heard her mother whisper words of love, of comfort. She saw Anna's sad smile as she tried to chase away the fear for both of them. She felt Anna's arms, filled with warmth and hope, wrapping around her. In the dream, Aubrey hugged her mother just as tightly.

When she woke, she felt lighter, as if a heavy weight were lifted from her shoulders. She didn't understand, but a tiny fragment of the anger she'd carried for so long had vanished.

CHAPTER TWENTY-THREE

B y the time Aubrey finally made her way downstairs, the sky had grown dark. She'd spent the remainder of the day in her room, too angry and confused to face the Bonaventures. She didn't trust herself not to hurl vicious words at Mrs. Bonaventure, and she had no idea what to say to Anson. The caretakers were her grandparents, and Anson was her father. The concept was mind-boggling.

She didn't know how to handle the news, so she pushed it into the far corners of her mind where all the painful things lived and went into the kitchen to fix a snack. Spectre rubbed against her legs and purred. Aubrey stooped down to pet her.

"Why did I ever come to this place, Spectre? Nothing good has happened since I walked through that door," she said quietly.

Spectre meowed loudly and tilted her head.

"Well, nothing good besides meeting you, I mean," she corrected herself.

Aubrey's telephone buzzed on the counter beside her, and the jarring sound caused her to nearly jump out of her skin. She glanced at the display and saw it was Hank.

"Hello," she answered tentatively.

"Hey, Aubrey. I was just calling to check in on you. How are you doing?"

His calm, soothing voice reached through the phone line, wrapping itself around her like an old friend.

"I'm fine." She paused. "Actually, that's a lie. I'm awful. I've had a terrible day."

Aubrey didn't know what it was about the man that forced her to open up, but she couldn't help herself.

"I'm sorry. How can I help?"

"You can't. Don't worry about me."

"I do, though. The thing is, I've worried about you since the first night I met you. And don't ask me why, because I don't know."

"You have?"

No one had ever worried about her before. Knowing Hank cared enough to worry made her feel things she'd never experienced.

"I spend far too much time worrying about you, Aubrey. I probably shouldn't admit that, but there you have it. I think the Ross-Metzger connection must be programmed into my genetics or something."

Aubrey didn't know how to respond, which led to an awkward silence that neither person knew how to fill. After a few seconds, Hank spoke again.

"I also called because I've done a bit of investigating to

see if I could find more information about your family."

"And you found something?" Aubrey couldn't believe Hank had taken the time to dig up material for her.

"I talked to Clara Millburn at the library."

"I've been meaning to make an appointment with her, but I haven't yet. What did she have to say?"

"Clara has tons of records, which you're going to want to go through yourself. I barely had time to scratch the surface, but there was one thing that caught my attention," Hank began.

"What was it?"

"Do you drink coffee?"

"What?"

"Coffee. You know, black stuff, full of caffeine. Do you drink it?"

"Yes, I love coffee. Why?"

"Do you have any?"

"I always have coffee."

"Do you think you could brew a pot? Maybe I could come over, and we could talk about it in person?" His voice sounded hopeful.

"You mean now?"

"Yeah, I mean now."

"I guess so. But don't expect much from me, because I'm a mess. I slept all afternoon. Today's been a hard one."

"I have no expectations, and I promise not to stay too long, but I think I should deliver this message in person."

"All right. I'll put on the coffee and see you soon."

Aubrey hung up the phone and started the coffeepot.

She couldn't believe she'd agreed to let Hank come over. The mere idea of spending too much time with him made her insides twist into knots. She was doing the very thing she'd warned herself not to do—getting close to Hank Metzger. She needed to call him back and tell him she'd changed her mind.

Grabbing her phone, she was prepared to dial Hank's number when she detected movement in the hallway. Instead, she dropped her phone into her pocket and walked toward the front door. When she reached the winding staircase, she gasped.

Marie Ross was standing on the second step from the bottom, wearing the same white nightgown she'd worn every other time she'd shown herself to Aubrey.

"Marie?"

Aubrey knew it was crazy to speak to a ghost, but she didn't care anymore.

"Nothing hidden ever stays," Marie said quietly.

"You've said that to me before. What does it mean?"

Aubrey didn't know whether or not the apparition would answer.

"It all ends with you."

"I don't understand. Please help me, Marie."

"The circle is complete. You must break the curse."

"I don't know how to break a curse. I don't even know if I believe in curses," Aubrey replied.

"Your destiny is entwined with his."

"Tell me what you mean."

"It all ends with you."

Before Aubrey could say anything else, Marie was gone. Like a vapor blown away by the wind, it was as if she'd never been there at all. Aubrey wondered if she'd imagined the encounter. She had no way of knowing.

There was a knock at the front door, and Aubrey knew it was Hank. She'd been too distracted to tell him not to come, so she would have to deal with the ramifications.

Aubrey opened the large door and gestured for Hank to enter. "Come in."

"Are you okay? You look pale."

"Like I've seen a ghost, perhaps?" Aubrey smirked at the irony of the situation.

"Have you?"

"More times than I care to admit. The coffee is ready."

She motioned for Hank to follow her into the kitchen, where she started a fire in the large fireplace and poured them both a steaming mug of the dark liquid. They took their seats in the cozy breakfast nook next to the hearth. Hank took a long sip and sighed with appreciation.

"This is delicious. Thank you for letting me invite myself over."

"Well, I changed my mind and was about to tell you not to come, but I was... distracted."

"By the ghost?"

"As a matter of fact, yes. And it scares me that you don't find that strange."

"I've told you before, this place is haunted."

"I can't tell which of us is crazier, Hank."

He chuckled. "Maybe both of us."

"Well, you can thank the ghost for being here, because I was going to tell you to stay home."

"I'm glad the ghost distracted you, because I wanted to come over. By the way, I've noticed that you do that often."

"Do what?"

"Change your mind. You did it the last time I tried to spend time with you too."

"That's what I do. I make decisions and then second-guess them immediately. I hate commitments."

"It's not a marriage proposal, Aubrey. It's just coffee and a chat," Hank teased.

"It might as well be," she mumbled. "Anyway, you said you had some information?"

"I do. I was looking through old newspaper articles and town records, and I came across something that caught my attention."

"Go ahead. I'm anxious to hear it."

"Desolate Ridge was built in 1819. Like Gramps told you the other night, Henry Metzger was in love with Marie, Marshall Ross's bride. What I didn't know was that Henry Metzger was the builder in charge of the construction of this place. Not only was he in love with Marie, he also built the house she would eventually live in with her husband," Hank explained.

"Wow. Poor Henry. That must have been really difficult for him."

"I can't imagine. But there's more."

"What else?"

"The money Marshall Ross used to build this house

came to him by suspicious means."

Aubrey frowned. "How so?"

"Well, the year before the house was built, Marshall's parents, Cullen and Ione, died unexpectedly. They were burned to death in their beds while they slept. It was eventually ruled as an accident, but it reeks of foul play. Their will stipulated their fortune would be split equally between Marshall and his sister, Eleanor. Not even six months later, Eleanor disappeared, and she was never seen or heard from again. Marshall inherited everything," Hank detailed.

"I'm no detective, but it sounds to me like those accidents might not have been accidents at all."

"Yeah, it's more than a little suspicious. Marshall might have killed his parents and his sister so he could have all of the money," Hank theorized.

"His wife also disappeared without a trace."

"You think he killed Marie?"

Aubrey couldn't decide if she should share what she'd seen. Something told her she could trust Hank, but she needed more time to decide. It wasn't every day that a girl revealed she talked to ghosts and had experienced another person's death.

"I don't know. It just seems strange that Marie left, that's all."

"I agree. I think we need to keep digging."

Aubrey's eyes widened. "We? You still want to help me?"

"If you want me to."

"Part of me wants to say yes, but there's another part that doesn't know how to accept help."

"Then you should tell that part to mind its own business."

Hank grinned, and Aubrey laughed out loud.

"Your laugh is nice. You need to do it more."

"Maybe. I usually don't have a reason to."

"I'd like to change that."

Hank's eyes locked on hers, and she couldn't look away. There was an undercurrent of familiarity between them that she couldn't deny. Marie had said, "Your destiny is entwined with his." Was she referring to Hank? Or maybe she meant Aubrey's father, Anson?

"You said earlier that you had a terrible day. Would you like to talk about it?" Hank asked.

"You mean talk about my feelings? I don't really do that."

"Okay, then don't talk about your feelings. Just tell me what happened to make your day so terrible."

"I found out who my father is," she blurted.

"And that's a bad thing?"

"I don't know what it is. I'm still trying to process it. Apparently, I also have grandparents who have known about me all along and chose not to say anything."

"That's a tough pill to swallow. I'll bet you're really angry and confused."

"Among other things."

"They really missed out, you know."

"Missed out on what?"

"On getting to know you. It's their loss, because from

what I've seen, you're an amazing woman."

Aubrey had never believed men like Hank Metzger existed. She let her eyes linger a bit longer than she intended.

"You surprise me at every turn. Do you know that, Hank?"

"I'm not sure if that's a good thing or not, but thank you."

"It's a very good thing. Don't worry."

Hank tore his gaze away. The last thing he wanted to do was leave, yet he knew that's exactly what needed to happen. She'd had a rough day, and she was vulnerable. She needed space to get her head on straight.

"Well, thanks for the coffee. I should probably be going."

He stood, took his coffee mug to the kitchen sink, and rinsed it out. Aubrey followed.

"Thanks for the information. Every little bit is helpful. I have to get to the bottom of this supposed family curse if I'm going to find some semblance of peace."

"Between the two of us, we'll figure it out."

Aubrey followed him to the front door, and a strange sensation came over her. Rather than being in a rush to see him leave, she wished he would stay.

"It means a lot to me that you want to help. I'm not used to having people in my corner, Hank."

"There's a first time for everything. And I'm definitely in your corner."

He reached out and took her hand in his, giving it a gentle squeeze. A magnetic, electrical current vibrated between their gripped palms. The surprised look on Hank's face told Aubrey she wasn't the only one who felt it.

"What was that?" she asked quietly.

"I have no idea. But I kind of liked it," Hank replied with a grin.

"Strangely enough, I did too."

Hank brought Aubrey's hand to his lips and kissed it softly before letting go.

"I'll talk to you tomorrow. Take care of yourself."

"Thank you."

Aubrey closed the door quietly and listened for the sound of his car as he pulled out of the driveway. Once Hank was gone, she locked the door and headed upstairs.

CHAPTER TWENTY-FOUR

Aubrey busied herself in her room in an attempt to exorcise the image of Hank from her mind. She had no idea what was wrong with her. She'd never formed such an attachment to another person, and the very idea of getting too involved made her nervous. She tried to remind herself that she wasn't into relationships, but try as she might, the image of Hank's face wouldn't go away.

She ran her fingers lightly across the top of her hand. She could still feel the warmth of his lips on her skin. She wanted to deny it, but the fact remained that she'd enjoyed it.

"Spectre, I don't know what's wrong with me. That man is bad news," she said.

The cat meowed and kneaded the bed beneath her paws before settling into a comfortable position.

"This is where you're supposed to tell me to stay away from Hank."

Aubrey's voice echoed in the room. Exasperated, she

flopped on the bed next to Spectre. She rolled over onto her stomach, and something on the bedside table caught her eye. It was a very old locket, and it hadn't been there before.

With trembling hands, Aubrey opened it. The antique necklace was heart-shaped and delicate, containing a miniature painting of a man. It was Henry Metzger, but his face looked exactly like Hank's.

Aubrey knew with certainty that the jewelry belonged to Marie, who had no doubt kept it as a reminder of her love for Henry. She didn't know why it appeared at that exact moment, when she was contemplating her attachment to Hank, who was identical to the man in the locket. Perhaps it was a sign.

"What are you trying to tell me, Marie?"

Aubrey fondled the locket for a bit longer before placing it in the drawer next to the pearl necklace. She'd slipped the rose between the pages of a book to dry. She needed to keep the unexplainable, tangible mementos to convince herself she wasn't hallucinating.

Her shoulders and neck knotted with tension. She rotated her head in an attempt to loosen the kinks, but it was no use. She needed a hot bath if she had any hope of relaxing.

Aubrey headed into the adjoining bathroom and turned on the faucet in the large claw-foot bathtub. She drizzled bubble bath beneath the running water and watched as it foamed. She couldn't believe she'd waited so long to run herself a bath in the extra-deep antique tub.

As the water rose, she stripped away her clothes and immersed her body, sinking beneath the froth. Easing lower until she rested her head on the back of the tub, she closed her eyes and sighed, attempting to clear her mind of all thoughts of Hank.

After several moments, she was successful. Her body relaxed, the tension drifting away in the hot water. Her mind faded in and out of consciousness. She wasn't awake, but she wasn't asleep. She was in some sort of blissful in-between. She heard the faint sounds of an old jazz song playing in the other room.

Suddenly, her eyes flew open as her head was shoved beneath the water. She struggled to pull herself to the surface, but she couldn't. There was no one standing above her, yet the weight of a large hand was firmly planted on the top of her head, plunging her into the depths of the water. Her arms flailed, fingers wriggling to grasp the edge of the bathtub, then slipping away, unable to get a grip.

The room grew dark, then light again. Aubrey was on the verge of blacking out. She placed her feet firmly on the sides of the tub and pushed her body upward with all of her might. The hand thrusting her down was stronger. She tried again, but the force shoving her beneath the water was substantial. She was too tired to fight it. Her drowsy eyes were made of lead. All she could do was close them.

Aubrey didn't know how long she was unconscious, but when she finally opened her eyes, she was floating listlessly in the bathtub. The water had grown ice cold. She shivered uncontrollably, although she wasn't sure if it was from the temperature of the water or the terror of what had occurred. All she knew was she needed to get out of there.

On shaking, unsteady legs, she managed to pull herself into a standing position. She wrapped the large bath towel around her trembling frame and glanced at her reflection in the bathroom mirror. Her skin was so pale it was nearly translucent. Her wet hair hung limply around her terrified face. Dazed, frightened eyes stared back at her.

Aubrey was freezing. She walked into the bedroom and rummaged through the dresser drawer, pulling out the warmest pajamas she owned. She tugged the garments over her body and wrapped a towel around her dripping hair, then climbed into bed and dove beneath the heavy down comforter.

Someone had tried to kill her. Someone had attempted to drown her in her own bathtub. She was afraid and disoriented, but even in her frazzled state of mind, she knew beyond a shadow of a doubt that it had really happened. She also knew the perpetrator was not a flesh-and-blood person. Whoever tried to kill her was not of this world.

Having no idea what else to do, she reached for her phone and called Hank.

CHAPTER TWENTY-FIVE

Desolate Ridge
1940

James Ross turned up the volume on the console radio. The jazz sounds of Benny Goodman filled the master bedroom. He glanced into the adjoining bathroom and saw Annabelle's nylon stockings hanging from the towel rack. His wife hung those blasted things all over the place. It was enough to drive him mad.

He flopped onto the four-poster bed and tapped his foot in agitation. Music blared throughout the room, and his head pounded in time to the rhythm. James tried to remember why he'd gone into the bedroom to begin with, but he couldn't recall. He muttered under his breath, cursing his failing memory. It was all because he couldn't sleep. It had been days since he'd rested. His brain refused to shut off.

The incessant ringing in his ears grew louder, and he squeezed his head between his hands in an attempt to stop the sound. James tried to concentrate on the beat of the music, but it was no use. The monster in his brain was relentless, refusing to let him rest. He was crazy, just like his father, Clarence, had been. As hard as James had tried to be different, he wasn't.

He unplugged his ears and, through the ringing, listened to Annabelle humming the song "I Thought About You" from inside the bathroom. Her voice was clear and melodic. Annabelle Fraser Ross could have easily been the jazz singer she'd dreamed of, instead of James's wife and Stuart's mother. James knew the woman blamed him for her deferred dreams, as she blamed him for all her unhappiness.

The sound of water sloshing sent his anger up a notch. Why was she taking a bath in the middle of the day? Didn't she have duties to perform? She was, after all, the mistress of Desolate Ridge. Annabelle shouldn't have time for such indulgent afternoon pleasures.

Their young son, Stuart, was sleeping down the hall in the nursery. Shouldn't Annabelle be close by, watching over him like a good mother? Not that James knew what a good mother did—he hadn't had one for most of his life. His mother, Elsie, died when he was quite young. But he imagined what she would have been like, and Annabelle just didn't measure up.

James had noticed a change in his wife over the last few months. She was moody and distant, and the only person who could make her smile was little Stuart. She always flinched when James touched her, and his wife avoided him whenever possible. In a house as large as Desolate Ridge, that wasn't difficult to do.

Annabelle's moodiness angered James. She demeaned him, making him beg for her attention and then refusing him. The silly woman was probably still upset about the broken bones he'd given her after their last argument. Perhaps he'd gotten carried away, but he couldn't help it. Annabelle pushed him, and he blew a fuse. That woman brought out the worst in him.

Last month she'd told him she wanted a divorce. He'd convinced her she didn't. After all, members of the Ross family didn't do such things. They didn't divorce. No one in his family had ever divorced, and he wouldn't be the first. The Ross men always handled their problems without bringing the law into it. That was the way things were done.

When the doctor came to set Annabelle's broken arm, James said his wife had tripped and fallen down the stairs. It wasn't as if he was going to tell the actual truth. And Annabelle didn't tell the truth either. She knew what was good for her. She agreed to stay.

James swore it would never happen again, and then yesterday he'd lost his temper and smacked her across the face. The black eye and bruise on her cheekbone did nothing to diminish her beauty. That woman was too beautiful for her own good. Or his.

He'd lost his temper. Annabelle would go back to saying she wanted a divorce. That couldn't happen.

His ears began to ring again, even louder than before. He strode across the room and turned up the volume, trying to drown out the incessant ringing.

"I'm trying to relax. Turn that music down, James," Annabelle yelled from the bathroom.

"Don't tell me what to do! You're not in charge here," he screamed.

Any day now, Annabelle would pack her bags and abandon him. She would find another man and leave him in the dust. She would take Stuart, his son, his heir. That couldn't happen. He wouldn't allow it.

He glanced into the bathroom and saw those blasted nylon stockings hanging from the towel rack. The sight of them made his blood boil.

He turned up the volume even more. The music was so loud the windows shook. Even so, it didn't drown out the ringing in his ears. James stalked into the bathroom and stood over Annabelle's body, glistening beautifully in the tub. She glanced up at him, rolled her eyes, and then closed them again, blocking him out.

"Go away, James, I'm trying to relax while Stuart is sleeping. Can't you just leave me alone?"

Annabelle didn't open her eyes as she spoke. She didn't even have the decency to look at him. Why should she get to relax? He couldn't. He hadn't slept in days. James Ross had never been at peace. For as long as he could remember, he'd lived in turmoil, tormented by the monster in his brain.

Without a second thought, James leaned down and placed his large palm on top of his wife's head. He shoved her beneath the water and held her there while he slowly counted backward from sixty. Annabelle struggled, but her tiny frame was no match for his strength. Her eyes locked onto his, and he stared back at her lovely face as it blurred in the water. It wasn't long before her body stopped moving and her limbs grew slack. Her eyes were still open, looking at him, finally understanding that he called the shots.

James let go, and Annabelle's lifeless body floated to the surface. Her fingers splayed on top of the water, and he noticed the glint of the sapphire ring he'd given her on their wedding day. He knew he should feel something, but he didn't. His mind was blissfully blank. Finally he was numb, incapable of emotion. The rage was gone, drowned in the water with his wife. Maybe now he would get some peace.

Annabelle would have left him, and he couldn't let that happen.

He dried his hands on the towel, then grabbed his wife's nylons and tossed them onto the bathroom floor. He'd done nothing wrong. Annabelle had simply fallen asleep in the tub and drowned. It was tragic, really.

The song "Swingin' Down the Lane" blared from the console radio. James tapped his foot in time to the music as a wide smile bloomed across his face.

CHAPTER TWENTY-SIX

Aubrey shivered under the down comforter as she waited for Hank. She knew she'd been hysterical when she called him, but she didn't even care. Someone had tried to kill her, nearly drowning her in the bathtub, and she was afraid to be alone. Hank said he would come as soon as he could.

Not even ten minutes later, Aubrey heard him pounding on the front door. She rolled out of bed and ran down the staircase, flinging the door open. Tears coursed down her cheeks, and she didn't even attempt to wipe them away. She was too afraid to care what he would think, too frightened to be aloof.

When Hank saw the look of terror on Aubrey's face, he hesitated. He wanted nothing more than to comfort her, but he didn't want to scare her further by coming on too strong.

"Aubrey...."

"I don't know what's happening to me. Please help me," she sobbed.

Hearing the sound of her desperate, trembling voice,

instinct kicked in, pushing logic, reason, and propriety out of the picture. Hank pulled Aubrey close to him, hugging her tightly and stroking her back in slow, rhythmic motions, hoping to calm her. She didn't pull away. Instead, she folded herself inside his arms, practically melting her body into his, and let him hold her.

After several minutes, the tears subsided, and the pounding of her heart began to slow. Still freezing, her body trembled.

"You need to lie down, Aubrey. Let's go upstairs."

"Yes. I'm so cold."

She started up the staircase, but after only two steps, her rubbery legs gave way and she collapsed. Without a word, Hank picked her up, cradled her in his arms, and carried her the rest of the way.

"Which room is yours?" he asked.

She pointed toward her bedroom, and he angled in that direction. He gently placed her in bed and pulled the thick blankets over her shivering body. Once she was tucked in, he walked across the room and started a fire in the large fireplace.

"You're freezing. We need to get you warmed up. Once the shock wears off a bit, you can tell me what happened."

Aubrey didn't have the strength to speak, so she simply nodded.

Before long, Hank had made a cozy fire, blazing in the fireplace, the flames casting dancing shadows on the walls of the room. She felt her body beginning to warm. The trembling in her limbs subsided, and her weary eyes grew heavy.

Aubrey hadn't realized how completely exhausted she was, both mentally and physically, until that moment. She was tired of holding it together, tired of being strong.

Hank perched awkwardly on the edge of the bed. There were a million things he wanted to say, but he wasn't sure if he should. Instead, he remained silent, waiting for Aubrey to speak.

"Thank you for coming, Hank. I didn't know what else to do."

"I'm glad you called me. Can you tell me what happened?"

"I... I was feeling stressed after you left, so I decided to take a bubble bath. I got in, started to doze off, and the next thing I knew, my head was being shoved under the water. I know it sounds crazy, but someone—or something—tried to drown me. I fought back, but I must have passed out. When I woke up, I was afraid to be in the house alone, so I called you."

"Someone shoved you under the water?"

"Yes. I know it doesn't make sense, Hank, but that's what happened. I... I... don't have an explanation."

"I don't either."

"I also don't have any proof. It's just my word. My crazy, mixed-up recollection of what happened to me."

"I don't know what to say, Aubrey. But I know you're not making this up."

"You mean you believe me?"

"Of course I believe you."

Tears of relief ran down her cheeks as her body shook

with sobs. She hadn't anticipated Hank believing her. A part of her hoped he would just tell her she was crazy and get it over with. That would have been the most logical explanation. That's what she'd expected. But Hank didn't do that. He listened to her, tried to understand. He believed her, with no proof and no reason.

"I don't want to mess this up, and I know I'm about to, but there are so many things I want to say to you, Aubrey. I want... to hold you and tell you everything is going to be okay, that we're going to figure this all out together. I want to... be so much more than just your friend."

"You do?"

"Yes. But I don't want to scare you."

"I'm not afraid of you, Hank."

The words fell out before she could stop them, but she realized she didn't want to take them back. She meant what she'd said. Aubrey felt safe when she was with Hank, and at that moment, she would give anything for him to stay.

Slowly, Hank scooted closer to Aubrey. She inched nearer to him until they were side by side. She was still buried beneath the blankets, and he was on top of them, but that didn't matter. Hank angled his body next to hers and wrapped his arms around her.

She turned toward him, tentatively placing her head on his chest. Hank's heart pounded wildly, and Aubrey's matched it beat for beat.

"Thank you for believing me, Hank. Even though none of this makes sense."

"I told you we would figure it out, and we will."

"I'm afraid. I almost died tonight."

"Just rest now. I'm not going anywhere. No one is going to hurt you on my watch."

Aubrey closed her eyes and leaned in to Hank. She was weary to the bone. It had been weeks since she'd slept well, never able to let her guard down for a moment.

The fire flickered across the room. Between the hypnotic warmth of the blaze and the comfort of Hank's presence, she drifted off into a much-needed sleep.

CHAPTER TWENTY-SEVEN

Aubrey's eyes fluttered open as morning sunlight filtered through the lace curtains in her bedroom. It took a moment to get her bearings, and more than a few seconds to remember why Hank Metzger was lying next to her, his body wrapped around hers.

He'd promised not to leave her. Those were the last words she remembered hearing before falling into the deepest, most peaceful sleep she'd had in months. She'd heard his words, but she hadn't expected him to follow through. She'd imagined he would stay long enough for her to fall asleep, and then he would go.

In Aubrey's experience, people said what you wanted to hear, but when it came right down to the wire, they didn't actually follow through. But Hank had. He hadn't left her. He'd stayed with her all night long, allowing her exhausted mind and body to finally rest.

She shifted in bed as she watched him sleep. He was unlike any human being she'd ever known. He was kind, gentle, considerate, and protective. He was true to his word, and he had never pushed her for more than she was willing to give.

Aubrey hadn't set out to fall for the man; in fact, she'd tried to do the exact opposite. But the truth of the matter was that, in spite of herself, she *had* fallen for him. Aubrey had feelings for Hank, and no idea what to do about it.

She'd never actually cared for another person before. She'd steeled herself against human connections, and for twenty-five years, she'd done just fine. Then Hank came along and sent her reeling, floundering in waters where she didn't know how to swim. Something told Aubrey that Hank was just as unsure, and somehow that prospect made the unknown a little easier to navigate.

Hank moved his body and opened his eyes, looking around the room as if trying to remember where he was. He turned his head toward Aubrey, and a look of confusion and concern covered his face. He pulled his arm out from under her head and sat up quickly, then jumped out of bed and walked across the room.

"I'm sorry. I didn't mean to fall asleep."

"You must have been tired."

"I only meant to lie there until you fell asleep. I was going to sit in the chair...."

Aubrey understood immediately that Hank was worried he'd spooked her by sleeping next to her. He was trying to justify the fact that they'd spent the night holding one another.

"Hank, it's all right. I didn't mind."

She allowed her eyes to linger on his for a moment, hoping they might somehow convey what she felt, since words so often failed her.

"You don't mind? I didn't overstep... or push?"

"No, you didn't. In fact, it's been weeks since I've slept through the night, so thank you."

"I just don't want to scare you. I know your life has been... well, hard. And what I think is okay might not be okay, and I just... I—"

"Hank, I know you're trying to do everything right, and you can't imagine how much I appreciate that. No one has ever worked so hard to understand me."

"I do want to understand you. I really care about you, Aubrey."

"I know. I finally get it. I see it in everything you do. That's why I feel like I can trust you, Hank."

"You trust me?"

"I've never said those words to another person, but I'm saying them to you. I care about you. So please, don't walk on eggshells around me. Not anymore."

Hank stared at Aubrey, trying to process the words she'd spoken. He hadn't even realized the depth of his feelings for her until that moment, but they had been growing, tugging at him since the first night he'd seen her.

There was a connection between them, powerful, innate, and seemingly predestined. It was something neither of them expected, but it was ostensibly written long before either of them knew.

"Your destiny is entwined with his."

The words Marie had spoken reverberated in Aubrey's mind, swirling around, finally taking root. Without a doubt, she understood the ghost was talking about Hank.

Aubrey scooted out of bed and walked slowly across the room to where he was standing. Tentatively, she reached out and stroked his cheek, feeling the stubble of his whiskers beneath her fingertips.

"I don't understand why, but I need you, Hank. It's like everything in my life up to this moment has been leading me to you," she whispered.

"I know," he replied.

Aubrey stood on her tiptoes and pulled Hank's head toward hers, touching her mouth lightly to his. When their lips met, something inside her heart shifted, as if it were a puzzle piece that had been waiting for that precise second to slide into place.

She pulled Hank's body closer to hers, the kiss gaining in intensity. Whatever reservations she may have had about getting involved with him vanished like a whisper in a sea of raised voices. Trusting him didn't make sense and went against everything she'd ever believed, but her future was somehow linked to Hank's. She needed him, and he needed her. Nothing else mattered.

She kissed him as if her very life depended upon it, because she had the sneaking suspicion that it did.

Marie's words grew louder in her brain until Aubrey was sure Hank could hear them too.

"Your destiny is entwined with his."

CHAPTER TWENTY-EIGHT

Several hours later, Hank and Aubrey were seated in the corner booth at Rebecca's Place. Neither had felt like making dinner, and they were both starving. Rebecca had raised an eyebrow when the couple walked in, but she didn't comment. Aubrey had a feeling her friend's silence wouldn't last long. She was right.

"Fancy seeing the two of you here. Together." Rebecca smirked.

"Rebecca," Hank warned.

"You have totally made my day." With a large grin, she placed menus in front of her brother and her friend.

"Easy, sis." Hank smiled.

"You guys were meant for each other. I could see it from a mile away."

Rebecca giggled, practically giddy, then grabbed her phone from the pocket of her apron. She snapped a quick photo of Hank and Aubrey.

"What are you doing?" Hank asked.

"You just look so cute together. I couldn't resist."

"Rebecca—" Hank began.

"Sorry, little brother, but when you're right, you're right. And I am always right. I knew this was going to happen all along," Rebecca interrupted.

"We haven't set a wedding date yet," Aubrey teased her friend good-naturedly.

"But you'll be the first to know when we do," Hank chimed in.

"You're perfect for each other. It won't be long," Rebecca predicted.

She kissed her brother on the cheek and told them she would be back to take their orders in a few minutes.

"I'm sorry about all that. You know she was just joking, right? My sister tends to get a bit ahead of herself," Hank apologized. "She means well."

"Hank, it's all right. Remember, no walking on eggshells."

"I'm trying."

"Rebecca's my friend. I know she was just joking." Aubrey reached across the table and took Hank's hand in hers.

"I don't want you to feel pressured by anyone."

"I don't." Aubrey smiled at him to reaffirm her words. Neither knew how to successfully navigate being together, but they had both decided they were willing to give it a try.

They perused their menus and made their decisions as Rebecca returned to the table.

"What would you like to order?"

"I'm going to have a repeat of that delicious french toast. I've been thinking about it ever since the last time I ate it," Aubrey answered.

"I'll have the cheese omelet and toast," Hank answered.

"Don't you ever try anything new? You order the same thing every time," Rebecca scolded her brother.

"Sometimes he tries new things," Aubrey chimed in with a grin.

"Point taken. I'll get your orders in," Rebecca laughed.

Aubrey and Hank handed their menus back to Rebecca. Aubrey was just about to say something to Hank when she had the unmistakable feeling that something was about to go wrong. She felt a prickling sensation on the back of her neck, and her eye began to twitch.

Glancing around the room, it didn't take long for her to spot the trouble—it was walking right toward their table. Cooper Lawson, the mouthy teenager who had given her a hard time in Lawson's General Store on her first day in Rossdale, stalked toward them with an angry look on his face. His frazzled sister, Cammie, the cashier, followed closely behind, presumably in an effort to keep him from getting into mischief. Aubrey felt sorry for the girl, always having to clean up her brother's messes.

"Sheriff Metzger, what are you doing with this woman?" Cooper spoke loud enough for everyone in the diner to hear.

"Cooper, are you out causing trouble again?" Hank gripped Aubrey's hand tightly.

"I'm trying to save you from trouble. Don't you know who this woman is? She's one of those crazy Rosses from

Murder Ridge."

"Cooper, stop it." Cammie placed her hand on her brother's arm. He quickly shrugged it off.

"You should listen to your sister, Cooper," Hank warned.

"What is wrong with you, Sheriff Metzger? You can't get involved with her." Cooper pointed toward Aubrey accusingly.

Aubrey watched Hank closely, gauging his reaction. He clenched and unclenched his jaw, and his chest rose and fell quickly. Cooper was making him angry, and she knew Hank wasn't going to keep his cool for much longer.

"Just let it go, Hank," Aubrey said quietly as she squeezed his hand. "It doesn't matter."

"Aubrey's right, Cooper. Let's go." Cammie tugged on her brother's arm.

"I'm not going anywhere," Cooper said defiantly.

"You need to turn around and walk out of this diner if you know what's good for you, Cooper Lawson," Hank gritted out through clenched teeth.

"You're going to defend a crazy woman who will probably murder you in your own bed? What kind of sheriff are you?" Cooper laughed derisively.

"The kind of sheriff who is going to haul your butt off to jail if you aren't careful."

"Look at this, everyone. Sheriff Metzger is dating the crazy Ross woman from Murder Ridge." Cooper directed his statement to the other customers in the diner while pointing at Aubrey.

Hank jumped up from the table, knocking over his water

glass in the process. He stood in front of Cooper, towering over the defiant teenager. Hank leaned down to Cooper's level, placing his face directly in front of the boy's.

"You need to learn some respect. Aubrey has done nothing to deserve this. Do you want me to tell your parents about that little incident you had a few weeks ago? I agreed to let it slide, but don't push me, Cooper, or you're in for a world of problems."

Cooper's eyes grew large, and he took a step away from Hank. Just as the situation began to de-escalate, others in the room began to yell.

"Cooper's right, Hank."

"Everyone knows the Rosses are crazy."

"Why are you getting yourself mixed up with one of them?"

"Yeah, they're not like the rest of us, Hank."

Loud voices chimed in from all across the diner, one after another, weighing in on the craziness of the Ross family and the horrors of Desolate Ridge.

"Enough!" Rebecca stormed out of the kitchen and yelled over the chaos in her diner. The room grew silent, and every head in the room turned toward her.

"How dare all of you gang up on Aubrey? Aren't you better than that? You know nothing about her, nothing at all about the life she's had to live. Aubrey Ross is my friend, and if any of you have a problem with her, you can get out of my restaurant and never come back."

"Aubrey isn't going anywhere, so you might as well get used to it. And if I hear of her having any problems with any of you, that person is going to have to answer to me," Hank added.

Murmurs of shame and whispers of apology trickled like a dripping faucet throughout the room.

"Come on, Cooper," Cammie said quickly as she pushed her brother toward the front door. Surprisingly, the boy followed.

Once everyone had gone back to eating, Hank let out a large breath and sank into the booth. Rebecca came over and joined them. Their eyes met Aubrey's, and she could see the redress coming before either of them spoke.

"Don't apologize," Aubrey warned the Metzger siblings.

"But, Aubrey—" Rebecca began.

"Don't apologize," Aubrey repeated.

"I can't believe you had to sit through that. It's not right," Rebecca insisted.

"I wanted to ram my fist down Cooper Lawson's throat," Hank fumed.

"Then you would've had to arrest yourself," Aubrey chuckled.

"How can you laugh about this? I can't even remember the last time something made me that angry," Hank replied.

"I'm ashamed to know those people," Rebecca sighed.

"Listen, you two, what just happened was nothing. Absolutely nothing at all. I've dealt with things a million times worse my whole life. Those people are afraid of what they don't understand, terrified of what they can't explain, that's all. That just happens to be me," Aubrey stated matter-of-factly.

"You're telling me you're not upset by what they said about your family?" Rebecca asked.

"Listen, from what I can tell, the Rosses have always been a little strange, and Desolate Ridge is a weird, creepy house. That part is true. And Hank, they're worried about you being murdered in your bed by crazy Aubrey Ross. That part isn't true, but they don't know that. There's no harm done, really," Aubrey explained.

"Well, we're angry for you, even if you're not," Rebecca interjected.

"I swear I'm going to punch the next person who says anything bad about you," Hank added.

"That's the best part of the whole thing. I've been ridiculed and made fun of my whole life, but today was the first time anyone cared enough to stand up for me," Aubrey told them with a smile.

"Well, I hope it doesn't happen again, but if it does, you can count on us," Rebecca assured her.

"Thank you," Aubrey replied.

Hank and Aubrey finished their meal in peace, receiving a few curious and apologetic glances from the other customers in the diner. After paying their bill, they walked around town as Hank showed Aubrey some of the local sights. It was the first time she'd seen more of Rossdale than Main Street, and in spite of herself, she had to admit it was a quaint little town. The thought of leaving was pushed further into the back of her mind every day.

It was getting dark when they headed out of town toward Desolate Ridge. All the frightening, unexplainable things that had happened swirled in Aubrey's brain. She didn't want to be needy, but the thought of spending the night alone in the house had her on edge.

Hank pulled into the driveway and turned off the car. He sighed deeply, and Aubrey could tell he wanted to say something but wasn't sure how to proceed.

"Just spill it," Aubrey said with a smile.

"What do you mean?"

"I mean I can tell you have something to say, Hank, so say it."

"How do you know I wanted to say something?"

"I can read you like a book."

"That's scary."

"You have no idea."

Hank sighed. "Okay, here it is. After what happened last night, I don't want to leave you alone. But I also don't want to tell you that, because I don't want to seem overprotective."

"Hank, I hate to say it, but you just told me."

"I know."

"Lucky for you, I'm terrified of being alone in that house. So I guess that lets you off the hook."

"You mean you want me to stay?"

"Yeah, I want you to stay."

"Okay. I'm glad we agree on that."

"Besides, there are six other bedrooms in the house. What are you worried about?"

"That's true," Hank agreed with a serious look on his face.

"But don't worry. You probably won't be sleeping in them."

Aubrey grinned, and the couple climbed out of the car. She grabbed Hank's hand and led him inside the house.

CHAPTER TWENTY-NINE

"I'll see you after work. Good luck today," Hank said as he kissed Aubrey quickly.

"Thanks. I'm a little nervous. I'm not sure what Mr. Lemon wants to talk to me about. The last time he was here, he ran off because I asked too many questions."

"Do you want me to stay? I can be a little late for work if I need to be."

"Nope. I'll handle this on my own. Thanks, though. I'll see you later?"

"I'll come over when I'm finished. It might be late," he hedged.

"Better late than never."

She kissed him again as he headed out the door. Once he was gone, she went into the kitchen to fix herself another cup of coffee. She sighed, content for the first time in her life. Things were finally looking up. Nothing strange had happened to her in several weeks, and Aubrey wondered if it had something to do with the fact that Hank was always around. He made everything better. He chased the darkness away.

Still, she couldn't help but prepare for whatever trouble was waiting around the corner. As much as she wanted to think otherwise, she knew it was coming.

The day before, Mr. Lemon called to inform Aubrey that they needed to discuss her financial situation, and she had a feeling the proverbial "other shoe" was about to drop. She knew little about money matters, other than the fact that she'd never had any. If she really wanted the meeting to end quickly, she could just start asking questions about the Ross family. That had scared the attorney away the last time.

Aubrey had just finished her last sip of coffee when his car pulled into the driveway. She went to the front door and opened it, surprised to see Mr. Lemon wasn't alone. Mr. Wayfair was with him.

"Mr. Wayfair, I had no idea you were coming," Aubrey said.

"Yes, well, here I am. You're looking well. You seem to have settled in nicely," Mr. Wayfair replied with a tip of his bowler hat.

"It's been an interesting experience."

Aubrey wasn't sure how to describe her time at Desolate Ridge. It had mostly been confusing and frightening, but it hadn't been completely awful. After all, the house had led her to Hank.

"We have much to talk about. May we come in?" Mr. Lemon interjected.

"Of course. I'm sorry. I didn't mean to leave you standing

on the front porch. Come inside, please."

Aubrey led them into the parlor, and they all took a seat. Hank had started a fire before he left, so the room was warm and cozy.

"So, what did you want to talk to me about, Mr. Lemon? I have a lot of questions the two of you might be able to answer, if you have time," Aubrey began with a smile.

"First things first, we need to discuss your financial situation, Ms. Ross," Mr. Lemon said with a slight frown.

"You keep saying that. Is there something wrong with my financial situation? Am I poor again?"

Aubrey wasn't sure why she enjoyed making the grumpy old lawyer uncomfortable, but she did.

"You're not poor, Ms. Ross. Quite the opposite—you have more money than you'll ever need. But you should look at the financial records to see if there are any changes you'd like to make. Desolate Ridge has been run the same way for years, but it's yours now, so you should make those choices."

"Who usually makes the financial decisions, Mr. Lemon?"

"Your grandparents used to. Then your grandfather went into the hospital, and your grandmother became... unstable. When that happened, as their attorney, I took over. I've been in charge of the financials. But that job really belongs to you, Ms. Ross," Mr. Lemon explained.

"There's another matter to discuss as well, Aubrey." Mr. Wayfair leaned forward in his chair. "There's a nasty rumor floating around that you intend to sell the house."

"Where did you hear that?"

"That is of no consequence. The question remains: do you intend to sell Desolate Ridge?" Mr. Wayfair raised his bushy eyebrows and gave her an inquisitive look.

"I don't have an answer for you. When I first arrived, I had every intention of selling the house, but now I don't know. There are things I need to figure out, questions I still need answered."

"What kind of questions?" Mr. Wayfair asked.

"Questions about the Rosses, Mr. Wayfair. Questions about why the women in my family all died long before they should have, questions about why there seems to be an undeniable thread of mental illness running through my veins, and questions about how all of this affects my future," Aubrey replied.

"Some things are better left in the past, Ms. Ross," Mr. Lemon admonished.

"I disagree. I say this house has far too many secrets that have remained buried for years. And I intend to be the one who finally digs them up."

"You may not like what you find," Mr. Lemon warned.

"That doesn't matter anymore." Aubrey's eyes bored into the attorney, who seemed to want the secrets to remain hidden.

"I have a question for you, Mr. Lemon," Aubrey began. "If you and Mr. Wayfair had never tracked me down, what would have happened to Desolate Ridge and the Ross fortune?"

"It would have gone to your next of kin," Mr. Lemon answered.

"Like my child? But since I don't have one, then what?"

"Since you have no children, it would have gone to your next closest blood relative."

"Blood relative?" Aubrey asked.

"Yes, like your father," Mr. Lemon replied.

"But Anna never told anyone who Aubrey's father was, Mr. Lemon," Mr. Wayfair interjected.

"No, she didn't. However, Stuart Ross added an addendum to his will before he died. It stated that if no blood relatives could be located, everything would be given to the person he delegated," Mr. Lemon revealed.

"Who was that person?" Aubrey asked.

"I'm not able to tell you, confidentiality and all. It doesn't matter, though, because we've found you. You're the legal heir. Everything belongs to you," Mr. Lemon stated.

"That's sure to make this mystery person a little unhappy, whoever it might be. After all, because of me, the beneficiary Stuart Ross delegated will be missing out on billions," Aubrey theorized.

"Indeed," Mr. Wayfair agreed with a slight nod.

"Well, Ms. Ross, it seems you have some things to figure out, namely whether or not you intend to sell Desolate Ridge, and how you'd like to handle your financials," Mr. Lemon summed up.

"Yes, I suppose you're right. For now, will you continue handling the money matters for me, Mr. Lemon? I honestly have no clue what I'm doing, and you appear to. If you're up to it, I'd like you to continue," Aubrey offered. "I do have one idea I would like to tell you about, though."

"It would be my pleasure to help you, Ms. Ross. We will

talk very soon, and I promise to do my best for you."

With that, the two men stood. Aubrey rose from her seat, shook their hands, and led them to the door.

"I don't know what you're looking for, Ms. Ross, but I hope you find it. Like I told you in Seattle, I'm rooting for you," Mr. Wayfair said with a smile.

"Thank you. I won't stop until I have the answers. I promise you that."

The men left, and Aubrey locked the front door behind them. As she turned to go into the kitchen, she caught sight of Marie standing on the staircase. Knowing the ghost would speak to her, Aubrey waited.

"It all ends with you. Nothing hidden ever stays," Marie said as tears coursed down her cheeks.

"I know, Marie. I swear I'll uncover all the secrets of Desolate Ridge. I won't give up until I do."

CHAPTER THIRTY

Aubrey was sitting in the parlor reading a book when she heard a soft knock on the front door. She debated on whether or not to answer. It wasn't Hank; he would simply use his key to come inside. She'd spoken to Rebecca at lunchtime, and her friend mentioned a book club she was attending that night. They were the only two people Aubrey was interested in seeing, so she decided to ignore the intrusion.

Rather than leave, the person persisted, the knocking gaining in intensity.

Sighing heavily, Aubrey rose from her chair and went to the door. Swinging it open in irritation, she was surprised to see Anson standing on her doorstep.

It had been several weeks since Mrs. Bonaventure revealed that Anson was her father, and all parties involved had strategically avoided one another ever since. Clearly the evasion had ended.

"I'm sorry to show up unexpectedly," Anson said, refusing to meet her eyes directly. "Can we talk?"

"Come in," she offered, not knowing what else to say.

Nodding slightly, Anson stepped inside and, without a word, followed her to the parlor. Aubrey's stomach clenched with dread and anxiety. She'd known the conversation would have to happen eventually, but she wasn't ready for it. Of course, she'd probably never be ready.

"Have a seat." Aubrey gestured toward the couch, and Anson sat obediently. Uneasy, she perched in the chair across from him, wiping her sweaty palms on her jeans and hoping he wouldn't notice.

She finally allowed herself to look at him, the man who was her father. She had refused to think about it, avoided acknowledging it, knowing the moment she finally did would be one of the hardest of her life. It seemed the time had come.

Aubrey examined Anson's face, searching for any resemblances between them. She watched the way he sat, alternating between nervously clenching his fists in his lap and wiping his sweaty palms on his pants. She glanced down and noted that her posture mirrored his exactly. She let her eyes linger on the shape of his mouth, the slope of his shoulders, realizing they were the same as hers.

Anson Bonaventure was her father. She couldn't deny it, and she couldn't change it. There was nothing to do but face it.

"I rehearsed a speech on the way here, going over and over in my mind what I was going to say to you. Now that you're in front of me, everything is a complete blank." Anson cleared his throat and shrugged.

She watched him, nervously fidgeting on the couch, picking and chewing the skin around his fingernails. Aubrey did the same thing when she was nervous, and the sight of her father, a virtual stranger, mimicking her habits was too much for her to wrap her brain around.

A flash of righteous indignation punched her in the gut. Aubrey didn't know where the sudden surge of anger came from, but it struck fast and hard. It caught her completely off guard, surprising her with its unexpected intensity. It wasn't fair.

The fact that Anson Bonaventure could come into her home, sit on her furniture, and blatantly portray Aubrey's own subconscious habits was too much. She didn't even know the man. Why was she able to see every resemblance with excruciating clarity?

If his story was true, Anson was just as much a victim of circumstance as she was. Perhaps her outrage was misdirected. But Aubrey was bitter, and Anson was there, within arm's reach. Maybe it wasn't right, but at that moment, she flung her animosity at him, finally shooting her arrows of resentment at a flesh and blood target.

"I don't know what to say either, Anson, so I hope you don't expect me to." Aubrey allowed her frigid eyes to meet his. "Why are you here? I'm not sure what you want from me, but I don't owe you anything."

"Of course you don't. I wasn't trying to insinuate that you owed me something. I just figured that maybe we should talk."

"Is that so? How entirely appropriate that you get to call

the shots. That's been the story of my life."

"I didn't come here to upset you. I just want to talk."

Anson fidgeted nervously on the couch, clearing his throat several times and glancing helplessly around the room.

"Well, you're here. So talk," Aubrey demanded coldly.

"I know you're angry with me, and you have every right to be."

"Don't tell me what my rights are."

"I'm sorry. Aubrey, I swear I didn't know you were my daughter, but I blame myself anyway. I should have known. I should have figured it out sooner. I should have tried to find you."

Anson's voice quivered and tears filled his eyes.

"I loved Anna so much. If I had known you were mine—"

His voice broke, and Aubrey felt a sudden rush of compassion. Her bubbling anger, so prevalent only a few moments ago, was replaced with a tug of sympathy. The pain in Anson's voice was palpable. It wrapped around her heart and squeezed until it brought tears to her eyes. If she could see past her own pain, it was clear that her father had suffered nearly as much as she had.

"Look, Anson, I know you didn't make the choice to abandon me. That option was taken away from you."

She'd imagined the words would be excruciating to say, but they weren't. They fell easily from her lips. Absolving her father of his guilt was shockingly effortless. Aubrey had spent her whole life dreaming about the day when she finally found out who her father was. She'd imagined ways to exact revenge on the man who had allowed her to endure life as an orphan. But when he was there, right in front of her, all the horrible things she wanted to say didn't ring true.

The fact of the matter was that Anson hadn't abandoned her. He hadn't even been given the opportunity to do so. Her father had been denied all rights and decisions regarding her existence. They were both robbed of any relationship they might have had. It had been snatched from their grasp by a woman too afraid to do the right thing. If anyone was to blame, it was Mrs. Bonaventure, Anson's mother.

"I didn't come here to ask your forgiveness, Aubrey. As long as I live, I won't ask that of you. It's too much. I can't even forgive myself," Anson explained.

"There's nothing to forgive you for."

"Aubrey—"

"No, Anson. Just listen to me. You see, as much as I want to blame you, the truth of the matter is you didn't do anything wrong. You didn't have the chance to do the right thing."

"No, I didn't."

"But looking at you now, it's plain to see that you would have." Aubrey wiped away the tears that streamed from her eyes as they rolled down her cheeks.

"I would have been a good father. I swear to you. Everything would have been different if I had only known. I would have taken you and Anna away from this place. We would have figured it all out together. I would have given anything to be your father, to have a piece of Anna with me."

Anson buried his face in his hands and sobbed, his body shaking with every labored breath.

Aubrey didn't know what to do. She didn't understand the feelings tugging at her heart, cracking it open inside. She didn't know how to respond to another person's brokenness; she was barely able to contain her own. But she had to do something.

Timidly, she stood, walked across the room, and sat on the sofa next to him.

"Listen to me, Anson. I don't blame you. None of this was your fault."

She hoped her meager words could assuage his grief, because she had nothing else to offer. Perhaps in time she would, but the wounds were still too fresh.

"Thank you, Aubrey. I don't deserve it, but thank you."

"Thank you for coming to talk to me. I know it couldn't have been easy."

"I've wanted to talk to you since I found out, but every time I tried, I convinced myself it wasn't the right time. I just didn't know what to say to you," Anson admitted.

"I understand."

"I have no way to make up for everything you went through."

"I'm not asking you to."

"Aubrey, when I think of what you've had to endure, it makes me sick. I can't make amends for any of that."

"I don't know what the answer is, and I don't know how this works. But if I've learned anything, it's that you can't change the past."

"I would give anything to be able to change it."

"All we can do is start from now," Aubrey offered.

"Is that what you want? To start over?"

The hope in her father's voice nearly broke Aubrey's heart. If she'd been uncertain about a possible relationship with him, his expectant optimism changed her mind.

"I think I'd like that."

"I want that more than anything, Aubrey."

"I need to warn you that I'm brand-new at this whole relationship thing. I'm just learning what it means to have other people in my life. Don't take it personally if I don't always react how you expect."

Aubrey was open to exploring some type of contact with her father, but she needed him to understand that it would take her some time. If he was willing to be patient with her, they might be able to make it work.

"I promise not to push you, Aubrey. I'll be grateful for anything, because that's more than I ever imagined I'd get."

She smiled and tentatively placed her hand on his arm. He grabbed it, gripping it tightly in his own.

Anson cleared his throat. "I have something I want to give you."

He reached into his coat pocket and pulled out a small box. Aubrey noticed his hands were trembling as he opened it.

"I bought this for Anna a very long time ago. I wanted to marry her. I wanted that more than anything. I rehearsed my speech a thousand times, but the moment was never right.

Then she left, and I never got the chance. I'd like you to have it."

He pulled a small ring from the box and dropped it into her open palm. When Aubrey looked at the jewelry, her heart constricted inside her chest. It was a modest diamond solitaire set in white gold. She guessed it wasn't expensive, but she knew without a doubt it had been purchased for her mother with all the love in the world. The piece of jewelry was miniscule in comparison to the gigantic sapphire ring on her other hand, but the sentiment behind the two couldn't have been more different.

Aubrey placed it on her right hand as she met her father's gaze.

"I think my mother would be happy to know we finally found each other."

"I know she would be."

Anson rose to leave, and Aubrey led him to the front door. Not sure what to do, she gave him an awkward hug. The gesture was new and uncomfortable, but she hoped it conveyed her desire to start fresh.

Once he was gone, she went upstairs to her room. Hank wouldn't be back until much later, but she was exhausted from all the unfamiliar emotions.

She sat on her bed and let out a sigh. Glancing at the bedside table, she noticed a journal. Like all the objects she found there, it had appeared out of nowhere.

She grabbed the book and opened it, immediately recognizing the sloppy, slanted handwriting to be her mother's.

It was the same penmanship she'd seen on the suicide note.

Aubrey flipped through the pages, and as she did, a photograph fell out. It was a picture of Anna, who looked exactly like Aubrey, and a younger version of her father, Anson.

The camera had caught the young couple in the middle of a private moment. Anson was looking down at Anna, and she was facing the opposite direction. Pure love and adoration were written all over Anson's face, while Anna's conveyed confusion and sadness. The faraway look in her mother's eyes made Aubrey wish she could read Anna's mind.

Aubrey flipped through the pages of the journal and skimmed over one of the last entries in the book. It was dated 1994, the year she was born.

Aubrey is such a sweet baby. I don't know why my parents can't see that. They live to torment me. Their hatred knows no bounds. What kinds of monsters lock their daughter and granddaughter in a room in order to get their way? They want me to give Aubrey up, but I could never do that. She's the only thing that matters to me besides Anson, and my parents have made sure we can never be together. I have to get away from here.

Aubrey felt her mother's pain tugging at her through the pages, sensed the desperation and fear Anna had endured.

Wiping the tears from her eyes, Aubrey slipped the photo back inside the journal, opened the drawer of the bedside table, and gently tucked the treasure next to the rest of her mementos.

CHAPTER THIRTY-ONE

The next day, Aubrey pulled the BMW into the parking lot of the Rossdale Community Library. Hank placed his coffee mug in the cup holder and dropped his cell phone into his pocket. He'd been checking emails while Aubrey drove them into town, but he'd decided the task at hand deserved his full attention.

"Are you ready for this, babe?" Hank knew she was nervous, and he wanted to assure her that he was there for her, no matter what they might find.

"Yes. I've been putting it off, but I know if I want to find answers, I have to follow the paper trail."

"True, but I also know you're scared."

"I'm terrified. It's all becoming way too real."

"I know. I'm right here with you."

"Clara Millburn said on the phone yesterday that she has an entire section dedicated to Desolate Ridge and the Ross family."

"Your family is pretty notorious in this town," Hank chuckled.

"It seemed strange at first that there would be an entire section dedicated to the Rosses, but I guess since the town was founded by and named after my family, it makes sense for there to be a ton of records."

"True. I told you I barely scratched the surface when I was here before. It'll take months to go through them all."

"Well, I don't have months. I need to hit the jackpot a little sooner than that. I just have to figure out which direction to go with my snooping."

"Do you know what you're looking for?" he asked.

"I have no idea. I hope I'll know it when I see it."

"I'm sure you will."

"Well, that makes one of us."

Aubrey followed Hank into the library and shook Clara's hand as he introduced them.

"It's wonderful to meet you, Ms. Ross. Is there something specific you're looking for?"

"Oh, you know, just the usual. I'm hoping to find the information I need to break a family curse." Aubrey smirked.

"A family curse? I see…."

The librarian paused for a moment, as if contemplating Aubrey's strange words, then led them into the research room and gestured toward a large row of bookshelves.

"These are all files pertaining to Desolate Ridge and your family, Ms. Ross. I'll leave you alone to browse. Please feel free to find me if you have any questions," the older woman said with a nod and a smile.

"Thank you. I appreciate your help," Aubrey replied.

Hank and Aubrey looked at the mountain of information

and felt completely overwhelmed. They had no idea where to begin.

"Well, I did say I wanted information," Aubrey laughed.

"Ask and ye shall receive." Hank smirked.

They decided the best option was to divide and conquer. Hank started on old newspaper articles, and Aubrey opted for birth and death records.

Thirty minutes later, Clara stuck her head into the room. "Do you two have any questions for me?"

"I do, actually. I'm reading obituaries and death records, but I realize I have no idea where my family is buried. Do you know?" Aubrey inquired.

"Of course I know. It's my job to know." Clara grinned. "The Ross family members have always been buried in their private cemetery."

"Where would that be?"

"It's on Desolate Ridge property, located somewhere behind the house, my dear. Haven't you seen it?"

"No, I haven't. But I'm certainly going to go looking for it."

After two hours of perusing records, Aubrey felt like her head was going to explode. She couldn't believe what she'd found. The troubling information once again led her to even more questions.

"I've been scouring these birth and death records, Hank, and things just don't add up."

"What things?"

"Well, the causes of death for all these women are more than a little suspicious. For example, Annabelle Ross supposedly fell asleep and drowned in the bathtub, and Catherine Ross apparently died in an accidental fire in the sitting room caused by an errant candle. She tossed her young son through the window to save his life. Emilia Ross tripped and fell over the railing of the second-floor balcony, and the list goes on and on."

"I agree that their deaths sound a bit suspect. But just to play devil's advocate, it could all be true. I mean, people could actually die that way."

"I know, Hank, but…."

"But what? Is there something you're not telling me?"

Aubrey wrestled with the idea of revealing her vivid experiences with the women's deaths. Although she couldn't explain it, she knew she had felt them all die. She'd gone through each horrific moment in her own skin while seeing it through their eyes. Aubrey understood that each and every one of these women had been murdered.

"There's something I need to tell you, but I don't want to do it here. I'll make copies of all these records, and then we're going to go home, and I'll tell you a story you're probably not going to believe."

"I've believed all your stories so far."

"Yes, I suppose you have."

Aubrey made copies of all the pertinent information, thanked Clara for her time, and then she and Hank drove out of town toward home. The butterflies in her stomach reminded Aubrey of what she had to do. She needed to tell Hank about what she'd experienced, but she was afraid he wouldn't believe her spectacular tale. It was pretty far-fetched, after all, and there had to be a limitation to what a man was willing to accept with no proof to back it up.

She pulled the car into the garage, and they went inside. She rehearsed in her mind how to begin the conversation that would undoubtedly convince Hank she was certifiably insane.

"You didn't say a word all the way home. What's on your mind, Aubrey? You know you can tell me anything."

"I really want to believe that, Hank. But I'm not sure I can tell you this."

She busied herself in the kitchen making coffee while Hank started a fire. In usual Hank fashion, he didn't push her to talk. In fact, he didn't say anything. He simply sat at the breakfast nook reading the paper while she worked up the nerve to speak.

When the coffee had finished brewing, she poured them both a mug, carried it to the table, and sat down.

"Thanks, babe," Hank said with a smile.

"You know I'm stalling, don't you?"

"Of course you are. Take your time." He grinned.

"What I'm about to tell you is out there, and I mean it's so far out of the realm of possibility that I don't even want to say it out loud."

"You've told me some pretty unbelievable things so far."

"I guess I have."

"Remember when you said a ghost tried to drown you in the bathtub?"

"That's right. You already know that part, don't you?"

Aubrey had forgotten she'd told Hank the truth that night. She'd been so afraid, and it had all been such a blur.

"I promise to listen with an open mind."

"Well, just remember you asked for it."

"I'll remember that."

"What would you say if I told you the incident in the bathtub wasn't the only death I've experienced since coming to Desolate Ridge?"

"You mean that's happened to you before?"

"Well, not that exact thing, but…."

He wrapped her hand in his. "Don't be afraid of how it's going to sound. Just say it, Aubrey. You know you can trust me."

"Fine. The women I was talking about in the library? My ancestors? Well, I know their deaths weren't accidents because I've seen each one happen, Hank. I experienced the moment they were murdered, through their eyes, but in my own skin."

"Like when you were almost drowned? You were experiencing something that happened to someone else?"

"Exactly. See, I finally understand what happened that night. The records show Annabelle Ross fell asleep and drowned in the bathtub, but I know that's not true. She didn't fall asleep. Annabelle was pushed under the water and held there until she died. I know it, because it happened to me, except I didn't die. I saw it all through her eyes."

"Okay…."

"And not long after I arrived at the house, I was peeking over the railing on the second floor, and I distinctly felt two hands trying to push me over the edge. Emilia Ross died from a supposed accidental fall from the second-story balcony."

"Anything else?" Hank asked, eyes wide.

"Yes, as a matter of fact. The very first death I experienced was Marie's. I felt her being strangled when I was on the airplane coming to Rossdale. She was rocking her baby in the attic, and she was killed. I saw who did it."

"You've said Marie Ross has appeared to you several times."

"She has. She wants me to figure this out, Hank."

"I see."

"And remember the night I called you because the sitting room was on fire? Well, the records say Catherine Ross died in a fire in the sitting room after she tossed her young son through the window to save his life."

Hank shook his head slightly. "I hear you, babe, but that's…."

"Crazy. I know, Hank. But it's true."

"Have you experienced other strange things?"

"You mean besides the fact that I have regular conversations with a two-hundred-year-old ghost?"

"Yeah, besides that." He smirked.

"One day I came into the kitchen and found a muddy shovel propped against the kitchen sink. I was the only one in the house, and I didn't put it there."

"A muddy shovel?"

"Yes. It was really old and caked with fresh mud, like someone had been digging giant holes or something."

"That's bizarre."

"Also, strange objects keep showing up on my bedside table at weird times. Each one seems to appear when I have a question about something. It's like the house is trying to answer me."

"I told you this house was haunted."

"Then there was the day I felt absolutely compelled to go into the rose garden. When I got there, I was completely overwhelmed by a wave of sadness and grief that I still don't understand. I found six headstones that belonged to babies who died before birth." She looked down, the memory overtaking her for a moment.

"That's really sad and creepy."

"No kidding. I don't know what it all means. I have no idea where all of these things fit into the picture, but somehow they all do. It's like the house itself and the ghosts who haunt it are trying to tell me the truth of what happened to the Ross women."

"It certainly seems that way."

"You're saying you believe me, then?"

Hank smiled. "I'll always believe you."

"I guess the problem is I have a hard time believing it myself."

"It's not an easy pill to swallow. But maybe that's why you're here. Maybe the house has been waiting all this time for you to unlock the mystery."

"Marie's ghost keeps saying it all ends with me. You have something to do with it too, but I don't know what that is yet."

"Maybe you're the one who can finally break your family's curse."

"But what if I don't believe in curses, Hank? Isn't it a requirement of a curse breaker to believe there's a curse to begin with?"

He shrugged. "I have no idea. I've never broken a curse."

"I doubt many people have. I keep telling myself that none of this can be real, but the evidence keeps piling up in my mind."

"I feel like we're closing in on the answers. We just have to keep digging."

Hank leaned across the table and kissed Aubrey softly. She caressed his face with her fingertips and wondered for about the thousandth time how she'd gotten so lucky. She knew she couldn't do any of this without him. His belief in her bizarre stories gave her the strength to keep pushing forward to find answers.

Aubrey took a large sip of her coffee as Hank's phone rang. He spoke quickly, hung up, and rose from his chair.

"I have to go to work."

"All right. I'll see you later on?"

"Of course you will. I've barely spent any time at my house the past few months. Not that I'm complaining."

"I'm not complaining either. It's nice having you here."

Aubrey kissed him goodbye and walked him to his car. As she watched him pull out of the driveway, she made a spur-of-the-moment decision. She went inside, grabbed her coat, and put on her boots. Clara Millburn said the family's burial plot was located somewhere on the grounds of Desolate Ridge, and Aubrey knew the time had come to find it.

It was raining, but she didn't care. She pulled her hood over her head and tromped across the backyard, climbing a small grassy knoll and walking toward the rose garden. She felt the same intense sadness as she glanced at the trailing flowers, but she continued past it.

"I know it has to be around here somewhere," she said quietly to herself.

She walked a bit farther, and suddenly it came into view. Gasping, she spotted a black wrought iron fence surrounding a grouping of headstones. That had to be the Ross family's burial plot. She shivered as a thick fog rose from the ground below, obscuring the names on the stones. She needed to go inside the fence to get a closer look, but that was the last thing she wanted to do.

Her hand trembled as she flipped the latch securing the old iron gate. It creaked loudly, moaning like a lamenting widow as she opened it and stepped inside. She jumped as a crow cawed loudly. Glancing above her, she saw seven black birds circling over her head.

As she watched, six of the birds continued to fly in a ring, while one angled its body to land, came to a stop, and perched on the fence. The single crow sat there, staring at her curiously. Aubrey trembled under the gloomy bird's close scrutiny. From somewhere in the recesses of her memory, the words to a creepy old nursery rhyme resurfaced:

One for sorrow,
Two for joy,
Three for a girl,
Four for a boy,
Five for silver,
Six for gold,
Seven for a secret never to be told.

Aubrey shivered again. It wasn't yet dusk, but the dreary rain had darkened the sky, coloring the whole world in gray. The fog rested on the ground, giving the graveyard an otherworldly ambience.

Not wanting to spend an unnecessary amount of time in the cemetery, Aubrey took a quick stroll through the grounds, reading aloud the names and dates on the graves. She connected each one to the death records she'd discovered only a few hours before.

She also took note of the ones who weren't there—the women who had supposedly disappeared, vanishing into thin air. She didn't believe for a second that they had run away. There was more to their stories. Aubrey felt it in her bones.

She ran her trembling fingertips across each name, etched so permanently into the headstones. These women, her family members, had all died long before they should have. They had been robbed, taken from the world in the prime of their lives.

They hadn't had the opportunity to see their children grow. They hadn't understood the mental illness that clearly ran rampant through the veins of those children. They might have been able to help them if they had lived longer. They might have been able to alter the circumstances of the past. The women didn't live long enough to break the curse that had strategically strangled the life out of the entire Ross family.

But Aubrey was different. She was a fighter. Every difficult thing in her life had prepared her for this moment. She had survived unimaginable things, and she hadn't ever quit. She was determined to get to the bottom of all the secrets.

If it was the last thing she did, she would break the curse before it broke her.

CHAPTER THIRTY-TWO

Desolate Ridge
2016

*E*lizabeth Ross took a few labored breaths. Her eyelids grew heavy, as did her heart. Her burdened mind worked to grasp the fact that she was rapidly approaching the end of her life. There were things she had to do, reparations she needed to make. Her time was running out.

She rang the bell next to her bed. It didn't take long for the housekeeper to come running.

"Yes, Mrs. Ross, what can I do for you?"

"Call Mr. Lemon and tell him he must come immediately," Elizabeth demanded.

"Right away, Mrs. Ross."

The fearful woman scurried away like a scared little mouse. Elizabeth Waterford Ross had that effect on people. She demanded respect, and she liked bending people to her will. She was cunning, calculating, and shrewd, qualities *which had served her well throughout her life. It was the only reason she'd survived.*

She glanced around the opulent master bedroom of the mansion that had been her home for the past forty years. She'd reigned as the mistress of Desolate Ridge since the day she married Stuart Ross. It was a role she'd been born to play. A weaker woman wouldn't have made the cut.

Elizabeth sighed, twisting her body in the mammoth four-poster bed. It was becoming increasingly difficult to find a comfortable position to rest. She closed her eyes and the memories began, just as they always did.

Her life had not been a happy one. Her marriage to Stuart had been anything but blissful. Their partnership hadn't been filled with love and longing. There had been no romance. Instead, their union was comprised of power and wealth, status and prestige.

Elizabeth consoled herself with the idea that position was better than passion. Now that she was nearing the end of her days, she was less convinced. Having grown up listening to the stories about the women in the Ross family, she'd heard the whispers, the rumors floating about town, saying the Ross brides were cursed.

In the secret places of her heart, she believed the tales were true, but that hadn't stopped her. She'd always had her own agenda. So she had pushed the thoughts to the back of her mind where they belonged. She couldn't give credence to such things if she hoped to reach her goals.

People warned Elizabeth that Stuart was crazy. They reminded her that no woman who married into the Ross family lived past the age of twenty-five. They cautioned her that these helpless women all died too soon, leaving behind their young sons, always sons. Elizabeth had been forewarned. And she'd proceeded anyway.

In Elizabeth's opinion, the problem was that the Ross men always married women who were purely ornamental. They were nothing but trophies, women selected merely for their beauty. Elizabeth was beautiful, but there was more to her than just a pretty face. She possessed a hardness that gave her an edge, a sharpness that made her astute. The reason those vapid Ross women died young came down to one fact—they weren't intelligent enough to stay alive.

Intellect had never been a problem for her. Elizabeth Waterford Ross was smarter and more ruthless than any man she'd ever known.

She laughed indignantly to herself as her voice echoed in the large room.

"Stuart Ross had no clue what he was getting himself into when he married me. I wasn't like those other women."

Her laughter turned to bitterness as she continued her dismal trip down memory lane. She propped herself up in the bed, stuffing the pillows behind her frail body for support. Sighing heavily, she allowed herself to remember.

The real problems began a year after she married Stuart, on the day she delivered their first child. Her husband flew into a rage, irate because she'd given birth to a daughter.

"The men in the Ross family only have sons. It's a fact of life," Stuart had screamed.

He believed his lack of a male heir to carry on the Ross

name was Elizabeth's fault. He told her it was because of her inferior genes. So he doubled up his fist and punched her in the face, blackening his wife's eye only minutes after Anna was born.

"That was the biggest mistake that fool ever made," Elizabeth whispered fiercely as she recalled the event.

She'd been surprised but not afraid. She'd tried to play nice, but at that moment, she decided all bets were off. Stuart Ross had grossly underestimated his wife's capability for anger. Elizabeth stewed in her rage for a few days, knowing she had to find some way to get even. She wasn't frightened; her husband's cruelty only served to ignite a fire in her.

It didn't take long for Elizabeth to plot her revenge. She refused to be anyone's doormat or punching bag. She was too wise to play that part. Stuart couldn't push her around and get away with it. Armed with a Machiavellian sense of justice and fueled by resentment, Elizabeth hatched the perfect retribution plan.

She put a little ethylene glycol in his coffee a few weeks after the incident. The sweet-tasting poison caused permanent kidney damage, but in her opinion, it was simply a reminder that her husband should think twice before crossing her again.

Elizabeth's heart raced as she remembered what she'd done. She could feel the anticipation all over again, as if it had only happened yesterday instead of many years ago.

"Served that monster right," she said to herself as she smoothed her hands across the down comforter.

That day, Stuart learned Elizabeth was smarter and

more malicious than he could ever be. She warned him to watch his back, assuring him she would always be one step ahead of him.

Perhaps she was mentally unstable. It was possible. People had called her crazy her whole life, but Elizabeth didn't care. Maybe she was a little erratic, a bit deranged. None of that mattered. So what if she saw visions and heard voices; her premonitions were what kept her alive. Stuart Ross deserved everything he'd gotten.

Elizabeth twisted the sapphire ring on her left hand as her thoughts turned dark. Tears filled her eyes, and sadness washed over her.

"I don't want to remember, but I have to," she whispered in a ragged voice. "I must face it."

Sadly, motherhood hadn't agreed with Elizabeth. She just didn't have the emotional capability or maternal instinct required for the tedious task of raising a child. Producing offspring was her duty, and she'd fulfilled it, but her obligation went no further than that.

Elizabeth felt no connection at all to Anna. She tried, but she believed herself incapable of such feelings. For the most part, she left the child-rearing to the maids. It was better that way.

Stuart, on the other hand, was downright cruel to their daughter. He tortured her, both emotionally and physically. There were a few times Elizabeth considered stepping in and telling her husband he was out of line, but the moments were always fleeting. Besides, Elizabeth believed hardship created strength, and she didn't intend to be the mother of a weak daughter.

Elizabeth rarely interfered with Stuart's parenting style, not even when he insisted they imprison their daughter and grandchild. Anna's pregnancy was a disgrace to the family, after all, and the problem had to be taken care of. They intended to put an end to the father as well, but her daughter refused to confess his name.

Anna was only a child herself. She had no business trying to be a mother. Forcing the girl's hand into giving up the baby had really been the only option. But their plan had backfired.

After Anna ran away with the child, Stuart had gone off the deep end. The man turned into a raving lunatic, and Elizabeth had no choice but to lock him away. He died in the mental hospital the year after Anna killed herself.

She didn't shed a single tear over the death of her husband. She'd never felt even an ounce of love for the man. He was simply a means to an end. She wanted his wealth and power, and she'd gotten it.

"Good riddance to bad rubbish," Elizabeth hissed as she took a sip of her hot tea.

Placing the cup on the bedside table, she relaxed into the pillows once again. She knew what was coming next. She knew the memories she'd unleashed. She couldn't forget the voices.

Her own descent into the darkness began when the paintings of the ancestors throughout the house started speaking to her, telling her she had to break the curse. It made Elizabeth angry.

After all, she believed she had already broken the curse. She was the first Ross woman to live past the age of twenty-five. She was the first to give birth to a daughter instead of a son. In her mind, she had done the impossible—she had outlived a Ross man.

But the paintings wouldn't stop talking. They laughed at her, ridiculed her, and demanded that she break the curse. When she told her doctor what was happening, he turned on her. He labeled her.

Schizophrenic.

Crazy.

Unstable.

Mad.

Insane.

"They wouldn't listen to me," Elizabeth muttered.

Still, the paintings spoke to her. She finally insisted the Bonaventures pack them away in the attic so she could get some peace. But peace wouldn't come. Tranquility was always just beyond her grasp. It seemed her wickedness had finally come home to roost.

"I brought it all on myself," she admitted.

Elizabeth began to feel remorse. She relived every horrible thing she'd done in her life, finally feeling guilt for her terrible deeds. She was consumed with regret for the way she'd treated her daughter. She'd imprisoned her own flesh and blood, torturing Anna, forcing her to flee with her young child.

She blamed herself, finally understanding that she was responsible for her daughter's death. She was the reason

Anna had committed suicide. She had perpetuated her child's depression and mental illness. She'd been cruel, doing nothing at all to help her.

She hadn't stepped in to stop the abuse; in fact, there were times she'd encouraged it. Elizabeth Ross was a monster, refusing her daughter the only thing she'd ever wanted—a mother.

Elizabeth knew she had to make amends before she died. It was too late to make things right with Anna. She was gone. But maybe there was another way.

She thought of her grandchild. She didn't know if the girl had survived, or where she might be, but if she could be found, perhaps she could finally do the right thing.

"I'm here, Mrs. Ross," Mr. Lemon said quietly as he approached her bed.

"Ah, Mr. Lemon, just the man I need to see. I have a task for you."

"What is the task?"

"Somewhere out there, I have a granddaughter. I need you to find her."

"Do you have any idea where she might be?"

"None at all."

"You know nothing?"

"Anna died in Denver, Colorado. That's all I know. Perhaps you should start there."

"Do you have any information at all about the girl?" Mr. Lemon inquired.

"All I know is her name is Aubrey, and the last time I saw her, she looked exactly like her mother."

"What should I do if I find her?"

"Bring her here. Bring her to Desolate Ridge. Convince

her to claim her birthright."

"What if she doesn't want to come?"

"You must convince her. Everything belongs to her."

"But what about—"

"Stuart will not have his way on this," Elizabeth replied defiantly.

"You're referring to the person he named as his beneficiary?"

"Yes, I am. They cannot inherit the Ross fortune. It's unconscionable."

"Stuart Ross insisted the inheritance was payment for services rendered, ma'am. He also stipulated that you did not have the authority to alter his decision. The only way to avoid it is to find a blood relative."

"Stuart Ross is dead, and if I have anything to do with it, his lackey will die with nothing, just as my husband did."

"I understand, ma'am."

"Good. Find Aubrey. Get Mr. Wayfair to help you. He's a clever man."

"Indeed. As you wish, Mrs. Ross."

Mr. Lemon turned on his heel and quickly exited the room, no doubt to begin the long, arduous search for Elizabeth's long-lost granddaughter.

The wheels had been set in motion. If Elizabeth had any say in the matter, the wrongs of the past would finally be righted.

"It all ends with you, Aubrey," she whispered as she closed her eyes and tried to sleep.

CHAPTER THIRTY-THREE

A week later, Aubrey was snuggled in her bed, warm beneath the down comforter, scouring the pages of *The Secret Garden*. The book had been her childhood favorite, and she'd found it on the bookshelf in her room. She had been happy for the discovery, especially after seeing her mother's name written on the front page. The fact that the book had belonged to Anna made it even more special.

With a sigh, she placed the novel on the bedside table and picked up her mother's journal. It was early in the morning, and Hank had already left for work. She knew she should try to get some sleep, but she felt restless. For the past few days, she'd known she was standing on the precipice of something big. She felt a sense of anticipation crackling in the air, although she couldn't explain why.

After finding the records at the library and visiting the Ross family cemetery, she was more determined than ever. Day after day, she continued working to uncover the mystery. In her mind, it was all coming together. She was getting close. She could feel it. The answers were right under her nose; she just had to put the last few puzzle pieces together in order to form a complete picture.

She flipped the page in her mother's journal and continued reading. A paragraph near the bottom of the paper practically jumped out and smacked her across the face.

I believe Desolate Ridge is cursed. The Ross family is cursed. But I know the curse can be broken. I've dreamed about it. I don't know what part I'll play in the unraveling of the evil, but somehow it has to be done. Sometimes I feel like the house is telling me what I need to do, whispering its secrets to me. The house has all of the answers.

Apparently Aubrey's mother had felt it too. Anna had also believed Desolate Ridge held the answers required to unlock the mystery. Deep down, Aubrey knew the house was the key. Everything she'd found was because of the house. Every scrap of history she'd unearthed was because the ghosts had made sure she would find them. All the mementos that surfaced had shown up at exactly the time she'd needed to see them.

"What am I missing?"

Aubrey spoke the desperate words into the quiet of the room, her voice drifting away like a feather in the breeze. She wiggled her finger and tried to twist the sapphire ring. Glancing down, she noticed the stone was glowing, an eerie light emanating from the piece of jewelry. It squeezed her finger tightly.

Like a lightbulb turning on in her brain, she realized the ring always grew tighter right before Marie appeared.

Sure enough, she glanced into the hallway and saw Marie standing there, dressed in white, her chestnut curls cascading down her back. Aubrey's eyes met the ghost's, and she understood Marie was trying to tell her something. She needed to pay attention.

Rising from her bed, she walked into the hallway, her heart racing a mile a minute. Marie paused, then turned and moved toward the doorway leading to the attic. That was the last place Aubrey wanted to go, but she knew she had to follow. Marie walked through the wooden door, vanishing through it like a vapor. Aubrey gasped, swung the door open, and started up the staircase. There was something Marie wanted her to see, something she needed Aubrey to know.

Marie was behaving differently, erratically. The ghost moved quickly, rushing toward the top of the stairway. There was a sense of urgency Aubrey hadn't felt before, so she took the stairs two at a time in an effort to keep up.

Goose bumps erupted on Aubrey's arms, and the hairs on the back of her neck prickled. Her eye twitched. The air was magnetically charged, trembling, vibrating with electricity. Something was happening. Aubrey felt it in her gut.

She stepped into the attic, flipping on the light in the hope of chasing away the darkness. She walked toward the middle of the room and stood next to an old rocking chair. She didn't remember seeing it the last time she was in the attic.

Marie moved swiftly across the room and stood in front of the window. She glanced back and forth, her gaze alternating between Aubrey, the rocking chair, and the wardrobes lining the wall. The message was unclear.

"I don't understand what you're trying to show me, Marie."

As Aubrey spoke, tears began to stream down Marie's beautiful face. The ring squeezed Aubrey's finger tightly. She looked down at her hand and noticed it was swollen, her finger nearly purple from the tightness of the jewelry.

Terrified, she grabbed the ring and tugged, trying to pull it off. She yanked and twisted, but it was no use. The ring was stuck.

"Help me, Marie. I don't understand what's happening."

Aubrey also began to cry, tears rolling down her cheeks. She stared at Marie, the ghost's face an exact replica of her own.

"Close your eyes," Marie said quietly.

Aubrey obeyed, squeezing her eyes shut as tightly as she could. She just wanted it all to go away. She wanted to go back to her life before she'd heard of Desolate Ridge, or Rossdale, or her crazy family. She just wanted the insanity to stop.

"Sit down," Marie instructed. "Sit down and see."

Aubrey sank into the old chair and closed her eyes once again. She began rocking slowly, back and forth in a sort of hypnotic rhythm. As she did, she felt the weight of an infant in her arms. The weight grew heavier, and soon she smelled the sweet scent of the baby's skin. She heard his steady, even breathing.

Aubrey opened her eyes and looked at the small baby cradled close to her chest. She softly hummed a lullaby, a tune she didn't recognize but seemed to instinctively know.

She stroked the baby's back, and the large sapphire ring glinted. She touched her mouth to the child's head, kissing him softly and feeling his downy hair beneath her lips. She jumped as the door creaked open behind her, wincing as she heard his heavy footsteps tromping across the room.

He stalked toward her, pulling the baby from her arms and placing him in a crib. The boy screamed, crying, wailing for his mother. Her heart broke into a million pieces. She knew it was the last time she would see her baby, the last time she would hold him in her arms. He was lost to her forever.

"Don't take my baby," she pleaded with him.

Her words couldn't permeate his insanity.

His face contorted with rage. He leaned in closely, and she smelled the scotch on his breath. His black, soulless eyes were nothing but a void. She opened her mouth to scream, but the sound was muffled as he gripped her neck tightly, his spindly fingers squeezing into her flesh and cutting off her air supply.

She couldn't breathe. She was going to die. This was how it ended. She understood now.

The man cried as he continued compressing her neck between his hands. Her breath grew shallow as her eyes fluttered open and shut. She was drifting in and out of consciousness; soon she would be gone completely.

"Why did you make me do this, Marie? Why couldn't you just do as you were told? Why does it always come to this?"

"You're... killing... me," she gasped.

She fought to keep her eyes open, trying to find a way to stay alive. He released his grip a bit and she wheezed, trying to force air into her lungs.

"Marshall...."

He sobbed, continuing to grip her neck as he squeezed with all his might. She struggled for several moments, but it was no use. Her body grew limp as she slumped over the arm of the rocking chair.

"You left me no choice, Marie."

Aubrey opened her eyes, straightening herself in the chair. She was still gasping for breath, startled by the stark reality of fully experiencing Marie's gruesome death.

Glancing across the room, she spotted Marie weeping beside the window. Aubrey sprang from the rocking chair, tripping over a box in the process. Her body thudded to the floor. As she lay there, working to catch her breath, she knew there was still something she was missing, some piece of the puzzle Marie was waiting for her to figure out.

Marie remained in front of the window, continuing to weep. The ghost glanced back and forth between Aubrey and the wardrobes lining the wall.

Tentatively, Aubrey rose to her feet, following Marie's eyes as they darted toward the wardrobes. She walked slowly in that direction, trying to understand. She looked back at Marie, who continued to cry.

Aubrey knew Marie wanted her to inspect the wardrobes, but she had looked through them before. It was where she'd found the paintings. There was nothing remaining inside but old gowns. But that was where Marie wanted her to look. She felt it.

Continuing to ruminate, Aubrey suddenly realized she'd looked through the wardrobes, but she hadn't moved them. Maybe there was something behind them she needed to see.

Taking a deep breath, she tried to push the first one away from the wall. But the antique piece of furniture was heavy, and it barely budged.

She tried again, funneling every ounce of strength she could muster. All she had to do was move it away from the wall. She pushed as hard as she could, and the wardrobe finally shifted. Aubrey wedged her body behind the furniture, using her feet to scoot it forward. After several attempts, she managed to move it from its original position.

She waited a moment, working to catch her breath. When her heart rate began to slow, she inspected the space behind the wardrobe. The area that had been hidden looked almost the same as the rest of the wall. *Almost.* Upon closer inspection, Aubrey realized a section of the wall seemed warped. She ran her hands across it, noting the texture felt different from the rest.

She looked at Marie again and the ghost began to cry harder, her body shaking with sobs.

Aubrey knew she had found where Marie was leading her. Something was in there, and she had to find out what it was. Frantically glancing around the room, Aubrey looked for a tool she could use to bust through the plaster on the wall. Seeing an old cane with a metal tip leaning against an ancient piano, she stalked across the creaky floor, quickly grabbed it, and ran back to the spot.

She raised the cane and began pounding it into the wall. Sweat dripped down her forehead and burned her eyes, but still she continued. The plaster began to break away, chipping, cracking, falling to the floor in small chunks. She banged against the wall harder, enlarging the hole she had made.

The plaster finally gave way completely, and a large section crashed onto the attic floor. Aubrey blinked twice, grinding the heels of her hands into her eye sockets, rubbing in disbelief as the dust settled around her. Her brain began to register what she was seeing, and the puzzle pieces shifted swiftly into place.

Aubrey's body began to tremble as the macabre discovery came into view. Wedged in the wall, propped between the strips of lath, was a woman's corpse. The bones were draped in scraps of a faded white nightgown, the remnants of chestnut waves still intact.

Aubrey opened her mouth and screamed, the sound emanating from the very depths of her core. She shrieked over and over again as the horror of the truth bobbed to the surface of her muddled brain.

She glanced toward the window. Marie was gone.

CHAPTER THIRTY-FOUR

When her howling finally subsided, Aubrey took several ragged breaths and tried to calm herself. She looked at Marie's corpse, unable to completely process the fact that the woman had been behind the attic wall for two hundred years.

No wonder Marie haunted Desolate Ridge. She'd literally been trapped inside the house, longing to be set free. Aubrey knew her discovery was monumental. In fact, it was a game changer. She had always suspected Marie had been murdered, and now she had proof. Marshall Ross had killed his wife and stuffed her body behind the wall of the attic.

The insanity she'd seen in Marshall's eyes had been real. The man was crazy. He had killed Marie. She hadn't vanished into thin air, leaving her young son behind, as Marshall claimed. Her body had been buried in the house all along.

As the wheels began to turn in her head, she realized

she'd made a breakthrough. If Marie hadn't disappeared, and her body was buried in the house, maybe she wasn't the only one. Maybe there were others. Maybe that was the source of the curse.

She shivered as the impact of her thought process came full circle. With trembling hands, she reached into her pocket, grabbed her phone, and called Hank. He answered on the second ring.

"Hey, babe, what's up?"

"Hank…." She tried to speak, but the words wouldn't come out.

"Aubrey, what's going on? What's wrong?"

"I… I found… Marie."

"I'll be there as fast as I can."

She hung up and dropped her phone into her pocket. Glancing back at the wall, she realized she couldn't stand to be alone with Marie's body for another second. She practically ran down the attic stairs, then rushed down the winding staircase and into the kitchen.

Heading to the sink, she turned on the faucet and watched as the water filled the glass. She guzzled the liquid quickly, trying to moisten her parched throat. Still shivering, Aubrey started a fire in the fireplace, then sat at the breakfast nook next to the hearth, waiting for Hank and willing the heat into her body.

"Aubrey, where are you?" Hank's frantic voice echoed down the hallway.

"I'm in the kitchen," she answered weakly.

He ran into the room, knelt in front of her, and took her

hands in his. "Tell me what happened."

"I found Marie."

"What do you mean, you found her?"

"I found her body, Hank. It's in the attic. She's been there all along."

"I don't understand."

"Two hundred years ago, Marshall Ross killed Marie and stuffed her body behind the wall in the attic."

"And you found her?"

"I did." Her voice broke and she began to cry.

Hank pulled her into his arms and held her. After several minutes, he spoke again.

"I know you're shaken up, but can you show me?"

"Yes. Follow me."

She slowly led him up the stairs and into the attic. Hank followed closely behind. As they entered the room, Hank gasped as he saw Marie's body wedged between the strips of lath.

"This is unbelievable."

"I know. This is what she's been trying to tell me all along, Hank. She wanted me to find her."

He pulled her close once more and rubbed her back soothingly, whispering that everything was going to be all right. She allowed herself to be held, thankful he was there and she wasn't alone.

"I'm so sorry you found her. I'm sorry you had to see it," Hank murmured.

"Me too."

"You know we're going to have to open an investigation, Aubrey."

"Even though it's been two hundred years?"

"Yes. We still have to connect all the dots."

"Okay. But now we know for sure that Marie didn't run away."

"Yes, we suspected it all along, but now there's irrefutable proof."

"There's something else, Hank."

"What's that?"

"Well, if Marie didn't just disappear and she's been here all along, maybe the others are here too."

"The others?"

"Elsie Ross supposedly vanished. Her body was never found. Then there was Eleanor, Marshall's sister. What if they're somewhere in the house too?"

Hank nodded. "You're right. We can't rule that out."

"So what do we do? How do we find bodies that have been hidden for years? I mean, I found Marie because she led me to the right place."

"True…."

"But Marie is the only ghost I've seen. I don't think that method is going to work for the rest of the bodies. And maybe they aren't here at all."

"We'll have to call in the cadaver dogs."

"That sounds awful."

"It's really not that bad. They know the scent they're looking for. If there are bodies here, even decomposed ones, the dogs will find them."

Aubrey shook her head. "I can't believe this is happening."

"I know, but we're on the right path now. We know what

we're looking for."

"This isn't any path I ever wanted to be on."

"Let's go downstairs. We'll have some lunch, and then I'll make the necessary calls to get the ball rolling."

Aubrey followed Hank downstairs, taking one last look at Marie's body before she left the attic. A feeling of deep sadness had lodged itself in her heart. She had experienced the horrible fear Marie had gone through right before she died. She'd felt the woman's heart breaking at the thought of never seeing her son again.

Marie was a part of her; her blood ran through Aubrey's veins. She knew she would never be the same, even after the nightmare finally ended.

Feeling numb, Aubrey robotically prepared lunch. Hank didn't seem hungry, and she had no appetite, but she needed to remain busy, to keep her hands from being idle. She was sure that's why he'd suggested she make lunch.

Hank made a series of calls, setting the investigation into motion. Within a few hours, Desolate Ridge was swarming with people. There was a coroner, a medical examiner, FBI agents, police officers, and of course, the cadaver dogs. Aubrey paced back and forth in the kitchen, watching the unimaginable scene unfold in her backyard. It seemed that every agency had a part to play in uncovering the two-hundred-year-old mystery.

When Aubrey grew restless, she went outside. The grounds were crawling with strangers. Not knowing where to go, she stayed close to the perimeter of the house, watching, waiting, trying to understand.

"We found something," a strange man's voice echoed across the lawn, and Aubrey saw Hank run in that direction. She followed.

"Right here. Let's do it," the man commanded.

"We have something over here too," another person yelled.

Aubrey's heart leaped in her chest. The dogs had found something—and in more than one area.

The crews began to dig, and Hank stood beside Aubrey, his arm wrapped securely around her shoulders. Aubrey lost herself in the shelter of his embrace and allowed her mind to wander. Time seemed to stand still. She had no idea how long she'd been standing there when a loud voice broke through.

"You're going to want to see this, Hank," someone exclaimed.

"I'll be back. You wait right here, babe," Hank instructed.

"No. I'm in this. I need to see. I have to, Hank," Aubrey insisted.

With a slight nod, he grabbed her hand and led her across the yard. On one side of the house, the dogs had located an area that held three bodies. Glancing down into the holes, Aubrey gripped Hank's hand tightly.

The corpses, which were clearly very old, had been placed directly into the soil, not buried in a coffin. There was nothing left but bones and a few scraps of clothing. All three skeletons had obvious evidence of skull fractures, and Aubrey immediately understood they had been bludgeoned to death. One of the bodies was larger than the other two, suggesting one was a man and the other two were women.

Aubrey began to piece everything together in her mind, immediately guessing their identities.

"Hank, I think I know who they are."

"Who?"

"I believe one of them is Eleanor, Marshall's sister."

"The one who disappeared?"

"Yes. I knew she never ran away."

Hank glanced back to the grave. "Looks like you might be right."

"And I think the other two are Ione and Cullen, his parents."

"Maybe. But didn't his parents die in a fire?"

"That was the story. But you know as well as I do that most of those tales aren't true."

"What if Marshall set the fire to his parents' house and made up the story that they died in it?"

"I think that's what happened. Look at the wounds on their heads. I think Marshall bludgeoned them to death and buried all three of them here, then told people his parents died in the fire and his sister ran away."

"That's as good a theory as I've heard yet," Hank agreed.

"Marshall buried his family in the dirt and then built his mansion right next to them." Aubrey's stomach churned as she came to grips with the extent of Marshall Ross's evil.

"He must have been insane."

"All he wanted was the money, and he had to kill them all in order to get it."

Hank nodded. "They'll have to run tests to confirm

everything, but I think you're on to something."

They walked across the lawn to where the cadaver dogs had made their other discovery. Aubrey gripped Hank's hand tightly as she looked into the ground below. There were two more bodies, presumably one male and one female. These bodies weren't as decomposed as the others, suggesting they hadn't been in the ground as long. Both had obvious fracture wounds to their skulls.

The smaller of the two was wearing a tailored blouse and skirt. The clothing, which had held up exceptionally well, was clearly expensive. It suggested wealth and privilege.

The larger one, the man, was wearing a button-up shirt, necktie, and military-style slacks. He had a gun holster around his waist. Pinned to his shirt was a sheriff's badge.

"The man was a sheriff?" Hank said quietly, his brow furrowed, concentration written all over his face.

"The only woman left unaccounted for is Elsie Willard Ross."

"She's the woman Gramps said my great-great-grandfather was in love with."

"The one who went missing?"

"Yes. My great-great-grandpa Howard. The sheriff."

Hank dropped Aubrey's hand and took a step away from her.

Aubrey immediately understood the nightmare that had been unearthed, as well as the ramifications. Elsie and Howard Metzger had been in love, but she married Clarence Ross instead. They had both disappeared around the same time. Aubrey knew without a doubt that Clarence had killed them both, probably in a fit of jealous rage, and buried them in the yard. With a sinking heart, Aubrey understood the impact of what that meant.

"Hank—"

"Your great-great-grandfather killed mine and buried him in the yard."

Hank's eyes met Aubrey's, and the pain and horror she saw reflected there nearly took her breath away.

"Hank, I—" She reached for his hand, but he backed away.

"I… I can't do this right now. I… I just need… to work. I have to work."

Without looking back, Hank stalked across the lawn away from Aubrey.

CHAPTER THIRTY-FIVE

Later that evening, Aubrey was in the sitting room alone. The house was dark except for the candles she'd lit, scattered throughout the room on various tables. Somehow, filling the darkness with candles seemed an appropriate way to mourn the deaths of the women in her family. They flickered, an unspoken remembrance of the souls who had been lost.

Aubrey had wanted to uncover the secrets of Desolate Ridge, and she had. The bodies had all been removed and taken to the lab for processing. Finally the house felt empty, truly deserted, for the first time since she'd arrived. The cadaver dogs had been brought into the house, but nothing else was found. It seemed everyone was accounted for.

Closing the chapter on the mystery should have brought Aubrey a sense of peace, but the dogs had dug up more than just the remains of her ancestors. They had dug up the truth, a truth including the fact that Aubrey's great-great-grandfather had murdered Hank's.

Hank had barely spoken to her the rest of the day,

refusing to allow his eyes to linger on hers for more than a couple of seconds. She had tried to apologize, tried to somehow alleviate his pain, but the damage had been done long ago. Even though she hadn't been directly involved, she carried a sense of responsibility that weighed her down like an albatross around her neck.

When Hank left, he'd told her he wouldn't be back that night. He'd made the excuse that he had too much work to do, but Aubrey knew better. The fact that one of her family members had killed his and buried him in the yard wasn't something they were going to be able to get past.

Whatever they had been building together was over. Hank blamed her, and he was right. Her family was crazy. They had schemed, plotted, and murdered one another, generation after generation. The Ross DNA coursed through her body, and eventually the curse would catch up to her. Why would Hank want to tie himself to that? No man in his right mind would.

Aubrey's phone vibrated on the table beside her. She glanced at the display and saw it was Clara Millburn. Surprised, Aubrey answered.

"Hello?"

"Hello, Ms. Ross. I'm sure you're exhausted after such a long and terrible day, but I've found something I wanted to share with you."

"You've found something else?"

"Yes. Do you remember the first day we met, when Hank brought you to the library?"

"Of course I do."

"When I asked you what you were looking for, you said you were trying to break a family curse."

"Yes, though I'm not sure why I said that. I suppose I was trying to make light of a difficult situation."

"Well, when you mentioned a curse, the wheels in my librarian brain started turning. I looked into the Ross family's genealogy."

"You did? What did you find?"

"I deal in facts, Ms. Ross, but I have to say that what I uncovered about your family gave me pause, to say the least."

"What is it?"

"I dug through the Ross family tree, back before they came to America."

"You were able to find that?"

Clara scoffed. "My dear, if it exists, I can find it. Anyway, Cullen Ross, Marshall's father, was born in a small village in Scotland in 1760. That particular village had a knack for exemplary record keeping. I was able to find a journal entry that was preserved in the town's records.

"You have my attention," Aubrey replied.

"Apparently Cullen Ross was quite a wealthy man, accruing his power throughout the years by questionable means."

"Why does that not surprise me?"

"Cullen's money and power led him to believe he could have anything he wanted, including the most beautiful girl in the village, Ione."

"That was Marshall's mother's name."

"Ione's beauty and kindness were apparently legendary, and Cullen decided she should be his. Ione didn't want to marry him, but Cullen persisted. He told Ione's mother, Annis, that he would marry her daughter, whether or not she agreed. Annis was the village wisewoman, and she didn't want her daughter marrying a wicked man like Cullen."

"I can understand that."

"One night, Cullen went into Annis's home and took Ione against her will."

"This is unbelievable."

"Annis, the village healer, was also considered by some to be a witch. Cullen and Annis argued, and Cullen killed her. Before Annis died, she cast a hex on Cullen, cursing both him and the Ross family. Because of his greed, Annis told him each generation of his family would be blighted. The Ross brides would all die young, and diseases of the mind would run rampant through their veins."

"That all sounds eerily accurate, Clara," Aubrey breathed.

"It's not a happy story, to say the least."

"Did you find anything about how to break the curse?"

"The story the villagers told said the curse could only be broken by one whose heart wasn't ruled by greed. When the circle was complete, it would all end."

Aubrey sat in silence, holding the phone to her ear, trying to grasp the threads of the unbelievable tale.

"Aubrey, are you still there?" Clara asked after several moments.

"Yes, I'm sorry. I'm still here."

"I know it's a lot to take in. It's a bit far-fetched, but I figured you'd want to know."

"I can't believe you were able to uncover that story. Thank you for sharing it with me."

"Like I said, if there's information to be found, I'll find it. I'm not one to put much credence in curses or ghost stories, but it was interesting nevertheless."

"Interesting is an understatement. Thank you, Clara."

Shocked, Aubrey hung up the phone. Clara's tale, seemingly nothing but a superstitious fairy story, had accurately described everything Aubrey had discovered about her relatives. She knew without a doubt that the Ross family curse was real.

There was a knock at the door, and Aubrey rose from her chair to answer. Opening it, she was surprised to find Mr. Bonaventure standing there. Although he had been in her house on an almost daily basis, she had spoken very few words to the caretaker, who also happened to be her grandfather.

"Hello, Mr. Bonaventure. What can I do for you?"

"I would like to have a few words with you."

His request and timing seemed strange, but Aubrey thought he was probably curious about the discoveries of the investigation. Or maybe he wanted to try to make amends with her.

"Come in."

She gestured for him to enter and led him into the sitting room.

"I apologize for all the candles. It's been an exhausting

day, and I was trying to relax."

Aubrey turned around to face Mr. Bonaventure, only to realize he had a gun pointed straight at her head.

CHAPTER THIRTY-SIX

"What are you doing? Why do you have a gun?"

Panic seized Aubrey as she took full stock of the situation. Mr. Bonaventure stared at her, his lip curled into a sneer. His steady hands gripped the gun, aiming the firearm directly at her.

"Why did you come back to Desolate Ridge? Why couldn't you just stay gone?"

"What are you talking about?"

"All you had to do was stay away. It wouldn't have had to come to this."

"I don't understand."

"You're just like your mother, trying to ruin everything."

Aubrey had no idea what was going on, but insanity was visible behind the man's cold dead eyes. He had clearly snapped. If she didn't want to meet a bullet, she needed to keep him talking. She had to find out what he knew, and why he wanted to kill her.

"What did my mother ruin, Mr. Bonaventure?"

"She tried to ruin my son's life."

"You mean because she got pregnant with me?"

"Of course that's what I mean, you stupid girl," he hissed.

"So you knew all along that Anson was my father?"

"Yes, I knew."

"You and your wife both knew, and you didn't tell Anson?"

"He didn't need to know. Your mother wanted to destroy his life. She got herself pregnant, hoping to trap him. The two of you would have ruined him. But I took care of it."

"You helped Stuart get rid of us."

"Who do you think kept you and your mother locked in that room? It certainly wasn't Stuart Ross. He liked to keep his hands clean."

"You knew Aubrey was mine, Dad? You knew, and you didn't tell me?"

Anson's voice sliced through the tension in the room like a knife. Both Aubrey's and Mr. Bonaventure's heads whipped around in surprise.

"Anson, what are you doing here?" Mr. Bonaventure asked.

"I came to talk to Aubrey. What are you doing here? And why are you pointing a gun at my daughter?"

"You need to leave, Anson. Turn around and get out of here. Forget what you've seen, son," Mr. Bonaventure stated.

"That's not going to happen."

Anson walked across the room and stood next to Aubrey, whose eyes were wide with shock and terror. He planted his body directly beside hers, standing so close that their shoulders touched.

"Put the gun down, Dad," Anson instructed.

"I can't do that, son. It's too late."

"What's going on in here?" Mrs. Bonaventure screamed as she ran into the room.

"Why are you here, Coral?" Mr. Bonaventure snapped at his wife.

"I knew something was wrong when you left, so I followed you. What are you doing?" Mrs. Bonaventure's voice shook as she took stock of the situation.

"I'm solving the problem. One I thought was solved a long time ago."

Mr. Bonaventure adjusted his stance and pulled the hammer of the gun, locking it into place.

"You don't have to kill anyone, Dad. What you did in the past doesn't matter. I forgive you. I forgive you for knowing about Aubrey and not telling me," Anson pleaded with his father.

"All she had to do was stay away. She made a mess of everything when she came back to Desolate Ridge," Mr. Bonaventure repeated.

"I don't understand. What did I do wrong?" Aubrey asked.

"You ruined everything!"

"All I did was what I was instructed to do. They told me to come to Desolate Ridge. They said that everything was mine," Aubrey stated emphatically.

"It shouldn't be yours! It was supposed to be mine!"

Mr. Bonaventure screamed.

Everything grew quiet as his words exploded into the room like a hand grenade tossed into battle.

Suddenly it all made sense. Aubrey remembered the conversation she'd had with Mr. Lemon. She had asked the attorney who would have inherited the Ross fortune if she hadn't returned. He told her Stuart Ross named a beneficiary, but Mr. Lemon was unable to disclose the name.

Mr. Bonaventure had worked for Stuart Ross his whole life. From the sound of things, he had been more than just the caretaker. He had been Stuart's cleaner, the man who made all of the problems and evidence magically disappear. In return for his years of service, Stuart had promised Mr. Bonaventure a fortune.

Then Aubrey showed up, not only bringing to light the fact that she was Anson's daughter, but ensuring Mr. Bonaventure would never inherit a cent.

"What are you talking about, Michael? Please tell me none of this is true." Mrs. Bonaventure's voice quivered.

"For years I worked for that man, doing anything and everything he told me to do. I never questioned him. I just did it. He promised me that someday, as long as Anna never returned, it would all be mine."

Mr. Bonaventure's eyes took on a faraway gaze. His hands, still holding the gun, began to tremble as he continued.

"I thought all the loose ends had been tied up when Anna disappeared with Aubrey. I thought the problem had solved itself. But then I got scared that the spoiled little brat would come back when she figured out she couldn't do it on her own. If Anna returned, I would get nothing."

"What did you do, Dad?"

Anson's voice shook as understanding dawned. Aubrey reached over and gripped her father's hand tightly inside her own.

"I did what needed to be done, son. It wasn't all that hard to find Anna, and everyone knew how troubled the girl was. It wasn't difficult to make it appear that she'd killed herself."

"You killed Anna? You killed the woman I loved?" Disbelief and pain enveloped Anson's words as he lashed out at his father.

"I did it all for you. You didn't need that girl. Or her daughter."

"No, Dad, no. Please tell me you didn't do it."

"They were standing in the way of our fortune. Don't you see, Anson? All of this was supposed to be ours." Mr. Bonaventure pulled one hand away from the gun and gestured around the room.

"You killed Anna for money?" Anson's voice dripped with sadness and disbelief.

"I would have given everything to you, you crazy old fool! I never wanted any of this. Don't you understand? I don't want it! You're as sick as my grandparents were. I hate money! It makes people insane," Aubrey screamed.

Fueled by anger, Anson ran across the room toward his father, slamming his body into the older man's. The impact knocked the gun out of Mr. Bonaventure's hand,

and it clattered to the floor, firing off a shot in the process. The wayward bullet sailed across the room, hitting Mrs. Bonaventure in the head. Her body slumped to the ground.

Anson scrambled to his feet and ran to his mother. He rolled her body over, but one look was all it took for him to understand it was too late. She was dead.

"What have you done? You killed her!" Anson sobbed as he cradled his mother's lifeless form in his arms.

Mr. Bonaventure stared in disbelief at his wife, limp in his son's embrace.

"I... I didn't mean for her...."

Mr. Bonaventure stood to his feet and paced back and forth across the sitting room. He ran his hands through his hair as his crazed eyes settled on Aubrey, focusing on her with tunnel vision. Aubrey was stunned, frozen in place, unable to fully take it all in.

"This is your fault. All of it. Everything that's gone wrong has been because of you." Mr. Bonaventure spoke slowly and deliberately as he stooped down, grabbed the gun, and pointed it at Aubrey once again. He pulled the hammer into place, and the clicking sound reverberated throughout the room.

Aubrey, too shocked to move, watched everything as it played out in slow motion.

As Mr. Bonaventure pulled the trigger, Anson sprinted across the room, flinging himself directly into the path of the gun, shielding his daughter's body with his. The bullet hit him straight on, ripping into his flesh. Stunned, he crashed into Aubrey, the impact bringing them both to the ground.

Anson's body smashed into the table, knocking over all the candles in the process. He landed on top of Aubrey, pinning her beneath him.

"No. No. No. Anson!" Mr. Bonaventure screamed.

In one swift movement, Aubrey saw Mr. Bonaventure look back and forth from his wife's motionless body to his son's. Without hesitation, he stuffed the barrel of the gun into his mouth and pulled the trigger. His large body hit the floor with a thud.

The flames from the candles spread quickly, and soon almost the entire room was on fire. Aubrey scooted her body out from beneath her father's. She glanced down at her clothing, realizing she was covered in blood. She didn't know if it belonged to her or to Anson.

Smoke billowed throughout the room, and Aubrey coughed and sputtered. She felt lightheaded as she noticed a large stream of blood spurting out of her leg. She had also been hit by the bullet.

She crawled over to her father and rolled his body over, placing him on his back. Resting her head on his body, she listened for breathing. His chest was moving up and down slightly. He was still alive.

Anson had taken the brunt of the bullet's impact. It had ripped through his chest, tearing skin and tissue, passing through his body before lodging into her leg. He was in far worse shape than Aubrey was. Her father had taken the shot for her, and he was paying the price.

The blood was gurgling out of his chest in a steady stream, a puddle forming around his body. Aubrey forced herself to choke down the bile in her throat. She had to help her father. He had lost so much blood.

"Anson... Anson, wake up. We have to get out of here," she pleaded as she ripped off the bottom of her shirt and placed it on his wound, applying pressure.

"Aubrey...."

"Yes, I'm here. But we have to get out."

Knowing she needed him to listen to her, she released the pressure on his wound and gripped his face between her hands. His eyelids fluttered open and he looked at her, locking his eyes on hers.

"My daughter...."

"Yes, yes. Look at me. Stay with me."

"Love you... so... much."

"Look at me, please."

"Anna...."

"Don't leave me."

"So... sorry...."

"Stay with me."

"Sorry... love... you."

"You have nothing to be sorry for. You saved my life."

Blood trailed from Anson's mouth and his eyes began to glaze over. The gravity of the situation nearly slapped Aubrey across the face. Her father wasn't going to make it. He was going to die.

Aubrey threw her body over his and sobbed. It wasn't fair. She'd spent her life without a father, and just when they'd found one another, he'd been ripped away from her once again.

"Stay with me. Please don't go. I love you… Dad."

Aubrey heard Anson take one last rattling breath. His chest rose and fell a final time, and she knew he was gone. She held him closely, not wanting to let go.

Aubrey began to cough and wheeze as her head grew light. She looked around the sitting room, now completely engulfed in the blaze. Her leg was bleeding profusely. She'd been so focused on her father that she hadn't realized she'd lost so much blood herself. She tried to stand, but when she put pressure on her leg, her body collapsed beneath her.

Losing her balance, she fell, hitting her forehead on the edge of the corner table.

Aubrey crumpled to the floor, her body lying in a puddle of blood as the smoke began to overtake her. She coughed and sputtered, her ragged breaths growing increasingly shallow. She touched one shaking hand to her forehead, feeling the blood pour from the open wound.

The flames grew larger, consuming everything in its path. She knew there was no escape. Her eyelids fluttered open and shut as she drifted in and out of consciousness.

She saw her mother, young and alone, cradling her closely as she ran away from the horrors of Desolate Ridge.

"I love you, Aubrey. I always loved you," Anna whispered.

"I know that now. I love you too, Mama," Aubrey answered.

Aubrey closed her eyes. Nothing had ended the way she'd hoped, but she finally understood her role in her family's story. She'd done her part. She'd found the truth and dug up the secrets. She'd unearthed the past.

She had broken the curse.

Aubrey's eyelids fluttered open again, and she smiled weakly as the women filed past her, one by one: Ione, Eleanor, Emilia, Anne, Catherine, Elsie, Annabelle, and Elizabeth. Each one smiled as she vanished into the smoke.

"I told you it all ends with you." Marie knelt beside Aubrey and caressed her cheek tenderly.

"Marie…."

"We are all finally free because of you."

When Aubrey looked at Marie again, there was someone standing beside her, a handsome man, clasping Marie's hand tightly inside his own. It was Henry Metzger, and he looked exactly like Hank.

Aubrey felt herself fading in and out of the blackness. She tried to focus on Marie, but the effort was becoming increasingly difficult. She coughed as her breathing grew shallow.

The crackling of the flames grew louder, and Aubrey knew the fire would consume everything, including her.

The shattering of glass in the distance caused her eyes to open once again.

"Aubrey? Aubrey, I'm here. Where are you?" Hank screamed loudly, his voice ripping through the roar of the flames.

"Your destiny is entwined with his," Marie said with a smile as she and Henry vanished into the smoke.

EPILOGUE

2021

Rebecca took a deep breath as she stood in front of the house. Everything looked exactly as it had before the fire. Desolate Ridge, now known as the Aubrey Ross Home for Girls, had been restored to its former glory. The blaze that had claimed the lives of both Hank and Aubrey had also destroyed most of the house.

It had taken several months to rebuild and properly staff, but in the end, the plans had all come to fruition. No expense had been spared, and the girls who would call it home had been painstakingly selected. The spots had been given to the children who needed them most.

"I'm so glad you could finally come, Rebecca," Mr. Lemon greeted her at the front door.

"Yes, well, I suppose it was time," she replied as she sighed deeply.

"I understand this is difficult for you."

"It's harder than I ever imagined."

"Hank was a good man."

"He was the best man."

"Your brother was a true hero, running into the fire, giving his life to try to save Aubrey's. He must have loved her very much."

"I think he loved her from the moment he laid eyes on her."

"I'm so sorry for what you've been through."

"In the end, I lost them both," Rebecca said as her eyes filled with fresh tears.

"You must miss your brother very much." Mr. Lemon touched her arm gently.

"I miss him every day. Aubrey too."

"That girl was like no one else I've ever met," Mr. Lemon agreed.

"I only knew her for a short time, but I loved her."

"Come inside and take a look around. It all belongs to you, after all." Mr. Lemon gestured for her to follow him.

Rebecca stepped through the front door and glanced around. The first thing she noticed was the painting she had commissioned, positioned prominently in the front of the entryway. The artist had expertly captured Aubrey's beauty in the portrait, from her clear blue eyes to her lovely chestnut curls. She wasn't smiling; that wouldn't have been true to character. But the expression on Aubrey's face exuded a sense of serenity and peace that made Rebecca smile.

"It's beautiful, isn't it?" Mr. Lemon said quietly.

"It's perfect. It looks as if she might walk right out of the painting at any moment."

"Indeed," Mr. Lemon agreed with a decisive nod.

Rebecca wandered through the foyer, running her fingertip across the marble end table that held a variety of costly trinkets and decorations. The crystal chandelier glistened, creating prisms on the ceiling as the afternoon sunlight danced through the elliptical fanlight windows on the front door.

Seeing the house completed was surreal, making it difficult to pretend nothing had happened. Ever since the night of the fire, Rebecca had tried to put the ordeal out of her mind. For months she'd been unable to face the fact that Hank and Aubrey were really gone. It all felt like a bad dream, and she'd been hoping to wake up.

The shock of their deaths had been followed closely by another surprise—Aubrey had created a will, leaving everything to Rebecca and Hank before she died. Since Hank had also perished in the fire, everything belonged to Rebecca.

"There are some papers I need you to sign, if you'll follow me into the office, Rebecca," Mr. Lemon said.

Obediently she followed the attorney down the hall and into his office, the room that had once been the parlor. Mr. Lemon was the overseer of the girls' home, but Rebecca owned everything and controlled all the finances.

"Have a seat," Mr. Lemon said as they entered the room.

He sat in the swiveling chair behind the large mahogany desk, and Rebecca settled into the plush armchair in front of it. Looking around the room, she was surprised to find

Mr. Lemon's office walls were lined with paintings.

"Those portraits look very old."

"They are indeed."

"Who are they?"

"It's every generation of the Ross family who lived in Desolate Ridge."

Rebecca's eyes widened. "You mean the paintings survived the fire?"

"Amazingly, yes."

"But how is that possible? I thought the damage was extensive."

"Well, the fire didn't reach all the way to the attic."

"The paintings were in the attic? I remember Aubrey talking about them."

"She found them there and brought them downstairs at one time, but thankfully she returned them to the attic. Otherwise they would have been lost forever."

Rebecca let her eyes linger on the faces of the people in the paintings. She saw traces of Aubrey in every single generation, but their faces showed none of the strength her friend had possessed.

"It would have been horrible if the paintings had burned. There's a lot of history there."

"Yes, quite a lot of history," Mr. Lemon agreed.

Rebecca fidgeted in the chair, trying to suppress her emotions as they rose to the surface. Suddenly she felt something against her leg. Jumping slightly, she looked down to find an inky black cat purring and rubbing against her.

"You have a cat?" she asked.

"That's Spectre. She's lived here forever."

"The same cat that lived here before the fire?"

"Yes. Don't ask me how she survived, because I don't know."

"That's very strange."

"I suppose so. I just need you to sign these papers, Rebecca. It's a detailed list of all expenditures for the renovations and the opening of the girls' home."

Mr. Lemon slid the file across the desk and handed Rebecca a pen. She glanced at the figures, the numbers swimming before her eyes, blurring together on the page.

"Do you need these today? May I take them with me so I can read them over in more detail?"

"You may do as you wish, Rebecca. You're the boss, after all," Mr. Lemon said with a nod.

"Yes, I suppose I am, aren't I?"

The idea that she had been left an enormous fortune still hadn't quite sunk in. Rebecca had more money than she could have ever dreamed, but she would give every single cent away to have Hank and Aubrey back.

She rose from the chair, slipped the papers into her purse, and sighed. She was anxious to leave but felt compelled to stay, suddenly realizing she felt close to Aubrey in the house.

"Would you like to take a look around since you're here, Rebecca?"

"Yes, I think I would like that."

"The girls are all around here somewhere. It's the

weekend, you know, so they have free time right now. You'll either find them in their rooms or out on the grounds exploring," Mr. Lemon explained.

"How many are there?"

"We have six who live here, ranging in age from five to twelve."

"And all the girls are orphans?"

"Yes."

"That's so sad." Rebecca's heart constricted inside her chest.

"It is unfortunate, but we're helping to rewrite their stories."

"I suppose we are."

"Aubrey made it crystal clear that she wanted a place where these girls could belong, a home for the ones who had no homes. She and I discussed it in detail weeks before her unfortunate death, and I prompted her to put it in writing. This was her vision for Desolate Ridge all along. I'm just sorry she isn't here to see it. It was very important to her."

"That's because these girls are just like her," Rebecca said softly.

Mr. Lemon excused himself, instructing Rebecca to make herself at home. He wanted her to feel like she was an integral part of what they had built, since it belonged to her.

Rebecca wandered back toward the entryway, meandering up the winding staircase toward the second-story balcony. The railing felt smooth and warm beneath her hand.

Rebecca peered over the edge of the railing, marveling

at how exquisite the home was. Happy sunlight flickered in through the clerestory windows, giving the place a peaceful glow. Glancing down the hallway, she peeked into the bedrooms, each one decorated carefully and beautifully. The cheery décor had clearly been chosen with young girls in mind. Each room was fit for a princess.

Most were empty, but she found one young girl in the largest room. The child was lying across the massive four-poster bed reading a book.

The little girl glanced away from the page when she noticed Rebecca standing there. "Hello," she said with a smile.

"Hello. I didn't mean to interrupt you."

"It's okay. Do you want to come in and look at my books?"

"Sure," Rebecca answered with a smile.

The little girl jumped off the bed, ran across the room, and grabbed Rebecca's hand in her small one. The child's red curls bounced delightfully as she led Rebecca to a large bookshelf and gestured proudly.

"These are all mine. Can you believe it?"

"That is quite a collection."

"When I came here, I had never seen so many books in one place before. Then Mr. Lemon told me they all belonged to me. It was the happiest day of my life," the little girl gushed.

"I've always loved books too. I can understand why you were excited," Rebecca agreed.

"What's your name?" The child turned toward Rebecca

and grinned warmly.

"My name is Rebecca. What's yours?"

"My name is Aubrey."

"Aubrey?"

"Yeah, I know it's a strange name."

"No, it's a beautiful name."

"I've never known anyone else with my name, and then I came to live in a house named after someone else called Aubrey. Weird, huh?"

"A little."

Rebecca's heart began to beat faster. The coincidence was more than a little odd.

"How old are you, Aubrey?"

"I just turned ten. My birthday is in October."

"Well, it's nice to meet you."

"I like it here. It's the nicest place I've ever lived. I hope I get to stay."

"I'm sure you'll get to stay, Aubrey," Rebecca assured the child. "You shouldn't worry about that."

"Do you know someone here?"

"Well, I guess I sort of own this house. It was left to me by someone I cared for very much. Another Aubrey, as a matter of fact."

"The Aubrey the house is named after?"

"Yes, that's the one. She's the lady in the painting downstairs."

"Oh, yeah, I've seen her. She's nice."

Rebecca's heart nearly stopped at the child's words.

"You mean you've seen her in the painting?"

"Yeah, in the painting and other places." The child shrugged.

"What other places have you seen her?"

"I see her all the time. She's my friend. Do you want me to show you my favorite book?"

"Your book? O-of course... I would love to see your book."

The wheels were spinning out of control in Rebecca's brain. What on earth was the little girl talking about?

Wiping her sweaty palms on her pants, Rebecca followed Aubrey across the room. The child grabbed a book from her bedside table, sat on the edge of the bed, and gestured for Rebecca to do the same.

"This is it. This is my favorite book. It's *The Secret Garden*. It says in the front that it belonged to someone named Anna."

The child placed the book, clearly well-loved, into Rebecca's hands.

"I always loved this one too," Rebecca replied.

"It's so good. It's all about hidden things and secrets. I've read it so many times, I almost have it memorized," Aubrey said with a grin.

"Can I ask you a question?"

"Sure."

"When you said you saw the woman from the painting in other places, what exactly did you mean?"

"Well, I see her everywhere—in the kitchen drinking coffee, in the sitting room reading, walking through the rose garden. I see her in my room a lot too."

Rebecca's breathing increased, her heart practically bursting out of her chest. The little girl must have been mistaken. Or maybe she just had an overactive imagination.

"I think the woman lives here," she continued.

"Why do you think that, Aubrey?"

"I don't know. She seems like she belongs to the house. The man does too."

"The man?"

"Yeah, there's always a man with her."

"What does the man look like?"

"He's really handsome, like a hero out of a book. And he has a kind face. He smiles a lot. The lady smiles all the time too."

Rebecca grabbed her phone from her purse and scrolled through the photos quickly. Tears filled her eyes as she stopped on the picture. She had taken the shot of Hank and Aubrey the first time they came into her diner together. It was the day she'd known for sure they belonged together. It seemed like a lifetime ago.

"Is this the man?"

Rebecca's hands trembled as she turned her phone toward the child. The little girl's eyes lit up and she smiled widely when she saw the picture.

"Yeah, that's him. And the woman too."

"And you've seen them here? Together?" Rebecca's body began to shake.

"Yes, they're always together, holding hands and smiling."

Tears began to flow down Rebecca's cheeks, but for the

first time in months, they weren't tears of sadness.

"And they both look happy?"

"They seem really happy. I asked them once why they were always smiling."

"And what did they say?"

"The man said he smiles because the woman loves him."

"Oh, Hank," Rebecca whispered. "And what did the woman say?"

"The lady said she smiles because they're together, and her destiny is entwined with his."

Thanks for reading *NOTHING HIDDEN EVER STAYS*. I do hope you enjoyed my story. I appreciate your help in spreading the word, including telling a friend. Before you go, it would mean so much to me if you would take a few minutes to write a review and share how you feel about my story so others may find my work. Reviews really do help readers find books. Please leave a review on your favorite book site.

Don't miss out on New Releases, Exclusive Giveaways, and much more!

LIKE ME ON FACEBOOK: WWW.FACEBOOK.COM/ HRMASONAUTHOR

FOLLOW ME ON TWITTER @HEIDIRENEEMASON

FOLLOW ME ON INSTAGRAM @AUTHORHRMASON

FOLLOW ME ON BOOKBUB: WWW.BOOKBUB.COM/AUTHORS/HR-MASON

VISIT MY WEBSITE FOR MY CURRENT BOOKLIST:
WWW.HEIDIRENEEMASON.COM

I'd love to hear from you directly, too. Please feel free to email me at HEIDISBOOKS999@GMAIL.COM or check out my website WWW.HEIDIRENEEMASON.COM for updates.

H.R. Mason is an Ohio girl transplanted into the Pacific Northwest. She is a homeschooling mom of three daughters, a wife of one mailman, and a people-watching introvert who can be found hiding out in the nearest corner. *Nothing Hidden Ever Stays* is her debut gothic suspense novel.

ACKNOWLEDGMENTS

This is the book that almost wasn't. When this story idea first came to me, I pushed it aside because I "didn't write that kind of book." After three years of ignoring the idea, I realized that rather than going away, the characters and plot had become even more vivid in my mind, begging to find their place on the page. Disregarding my self-doubt, I began to write, discovering quickly that no book had ever breathed itself into existence for me quite as effortlessly as this one. I'm so glad I took a chance.

I have a lot of people to thank for helping guide this novel into existence.

Christy Peterson, thank you for being the very first reader of *Nothing Hidden Ever Stays*. The way you devoured each chapter gave me the confidence to keep writing.

Cameron, my husband, thanks for actually reading this one. Your enjoyment of each chapter made me realize I was on the right path.

My daughters, thank you for understanding the days

when I was fully lost in my own head, completely immersed in the storyline. The way you believe in me and what I do keeps me going.

Chloe, thank you for helping me research mental illness. I wanted to do it justice.

Treena, thank you for using your talents to help me create the Ross family tree. Your passion for genealogy inspires me.

Tangled Tree Publishing, thank you so much for taking a chance on this book. Your belief in my work continues to humble me.

My tribe, your solid encouragement gives me a safe place to land.

Finally, this book was almost completely written in the corner chair at the office of Liz Borromeo Dance while waiting for my daughters' dance classes. That tiny space supplied the environment I needed to get the words on the page. Located in The Academy building in downtown Vancouver, WA, it is said to be haunted. Perhaps that's why the inspiration was strongest in that room.

ABOUT THE PUBLISHER

As Hot Tree Publishing's first imprint branch, Tangled Tree Publishing aims to bring darker, twisted, more tangled reads to its readers. Established in 2015, they have seen rousing success as a rising publishing house in the industry motivated by their enthusiasm and keen eye for talent. Driving them is their passion for the written word of all genres, but with Tangled Tree Publishing, they're embarking on a whole new adventure with words of mystery, suspense, crime, and thrillers.

Join the growing Hot Tree Group family of authors, promoters, editors, and readers. Become a part of not just a company but an actual family by submitting your manuscript to Tangled Tree Publishing. Know that they will put your interests and book first, and that your voice and brand will always be at the forefront of everything they do.

For more details, head to

WWW.TANGLEDTREEPUBLISHING.COM.